I0672168

Gem

City

Also by Shawn Michael Sullivan

Neon Burrito Publishing

Novella

Larry Angeles

Essays

Stormy Fortune

Short stories

Cosmic Robotics

One novelette two times

My Autobiography Is My Manifesto: Volume One [8.5x11"]
automanifest [5x8"]

A novelette plus additional material

Oscar Wilde's The Picture of Dorian Gray

Poetry

Frank Zappa & Barry Manilow
the name of this book is untitled but that's a bit of a lie
Eudaimonia

Baker's Dozen
Everything Within
Basic Mutant Psychosis

Copyright © 2019
ISBN 978-0-9985205-4-4

M,

Happy birthday.

S

This book takes place in the laws of fiction.

Shawn

Michael

Sullivan

Gem

City

A man who dreams is not asleep. You can't do everything at once.

Jean Ferry, "On the Frontiers of Plaster (A Few Notes on Sleep)"

Having expected to be already dead by this age, and feeling emotionally exhausted past his last work break, Tommy soothed his restless mind by remembering you only have to live once.

He had arrived at work chasing common interior demons that eluded him yet again, which tired him as always; followed by routine daydreaming. A child of darkness, he was standing there kind of working the register and kind of considering the adult world some absolute bullshit not worth head-on confronting when he noticed what always felt to him like a colossal mistake: Victor in another line with another cashier.

Seventy-six years-old and alone each time, Victor appeared to dislike bi-weekly shopping where thirty-four year-old Tommy appeared to dislike working, and in fact they each disliked everything, including disliking things. Owing to this instinctual observation Tommy considered their spiritual bond quite apparent, and adored becoming familiar with Victor.

To the average person look at Victor what the hell, what kind of strange man shops with like unspoken frustrations regarding everything.

To Tommy Victor was an exhilarating and highly relatable living symbol of one going forward however one does, without needing to feel great, but needing to keep going; wishing to be dead, but not acting as if dying; Tommy considered Victor a spiritual mascot.

Victor, meanwhile, did not think about Tommy, who was random to him.

And following a little over two years of Tommy cashiering, this afternoon Victor waited for a manager at the front of the store, while Tommy wondered what was happening.

It came to be that after the manager arrived, listened and nodded, then Victor handed over a notecard, followed by Victor leaving, and the manager posting the notecard on the bulletin board near the exit.

This filled Tommy with an immense curiosity he satisfied when off from work, cravingly reading the notecard's blue ink:

> Single bedroom
> No animals

No animals
589 McLain Street
Showing 12 p.m. Tuesday
[Reasonable price]

Comprehending the intention of the double-mentioned and once-underlined 'animals' sure made Tommy smile—though to be honest he did indeed feel as if he was a human kind of animal, the same kind as Victor actually.

Back then Tommy and a friend lived fifteen minutes away from his job, in a suburban Kettering apartment for two and a half years. Tommy had begun desiring to move closer to work, near downtown Dayton, and not just any place, but a place that suited his tastes.

Leading up to the showing, Tommy experienced supernatural feelings related to being meant for the room, instigated by Victor clearly being a kindred spirit. He had not implemented the internet as a means to investigate the home's physical appearance before seeing it, instead hoping for a real life delightful surprise.

On a peak-sun-activity summer Tuesday he made his way there, parking in front of a silver maple perimeter that obscured a clear view. And his desires manifested after passing these silver maples: this was a dirty and old two-story mixed-architecture Second Empire Victorian building, not too awkward or gaudy, semi-spooky, with a front-facing turret canted by bay windows, chipped and worn brick-red painted gutters —dreary, almost depressing, similar to a crack house —Tommy felt electric.

A true statement is Tommy felt better imagining himself living in this funky place than in some brand new and bloodless luxury glass apartment. Victor's house could be the setting for a horror movie, demons and goblins might live here, how neat, Tommy thought while climbing a short stack of stone steps that led to a walkway connecting to a second short stack of stone steps.

By the time Tommy was on the front patio, Victor's home was emblematic of Tommy's dreams. *Knock knock* and a minute later Victor at an open front door, an entry hall behind him.

First Tommy noted the home's surprisingly clean interior. And first Victor immediately did absolutely nothing: there was a long stale pause with no significance.

A skinny frail man whose hair had fled from his head, Victor wore a top-buttoned powder-blue dress shirt, a gold photo locket necklace, black dress pants, and polished black shoes: his usual attire.

Wearing a black t-shirt of a purple duck, grey dress pants and yellow sneakers, Tommy thought to say, "I'm here about the room."

Victor sighed.

Tommy shrugged.

Victor laughed.

So Tommy laughed too.

And Victor sighed again before saying, "I'd be surprised if you were here for another reason. Please wait on the porch until noon." He motioned to the porch before closing the front door.

Tommy's initial reaction: *Hilarious because whatever.* He hadn't mentioned to Victor that he took the notecard and no one else would be coming. There wasn't a chair so he sat on the cobwebbed dirty patio, which eww, but if that was the worst part of his day it wouldn't be too bad of a day at all.

Six minutes later Victor opened the front door again, checking for anyone else, no one else there of course.

Victor said, "If we hear the doorbell, you'll walk back and get the person," and Tommy grinned.

Victor led Tommy to the rear of the house, and not passing anybody along the way, Tommy wondered if anybody else lived here. Behind a door in the far corner of the kitchen there was a black steel spiral staircase, which Victor took slow steps up, with Tommy behind him.

At the top of the staircase they were at the end of a green wallpapered hallway and a grey wooden door which Victor opened while motioning for Tommy to enter.

It was a tiny housekeeper-like room, bare but for an open and empty trunk. Victor said, "The trunk is included." Tommy smiled, nodded, and wondered what else Victor might mention. The trunk was all that Victor mentioned.

Fucking staring at the room, Tommy experienced a growing affection: yes, he felt love. But did he? He experienced either a lust for newness or a lasting feeling while scanning the room with his eyes: a sunflower yellow ceiling, moss green painted walls, and pale wooden marked and worn floors. *Awesome* Tommy thought and then: would his affection for this place last another day, and a day after that—would he keep loving this room after it felt familiar to him? Could Tommy fill this room with his dreams he wondered. Did this room desire his dreams he considered. Would he be a benefit to this house and Victor, and would this house and Victor be a benefit to him, he pondered.

He decided to solve his questions by implementing the scientific method of the human condition: testing an emotional hypothesis upon a tangible reality composed by time; and Tommy was considering this when Victor, responding to silence, said, "Okay," and gestured toward the door.

Victor wasn't familiar with the simplicity of social manners, which Tommy thought was rad. Tommy felt comfortable. He knew he liked this place, and Victor had wanted other people enough to have made the notecard.

After Victor opened the front door he paused and said, "Well? There's nobody else."

Owing to personal conclusions Tommy had reached, he felt as if destiny was being offered.

Tommy moved into this home east of Oregon Historic District and downtown, in the neighborhood of Saint Anne's Hill, one of ten historic districts in Dayton, part of Historic Inner East, with nearly one-hundred and fifty buildings in Dayton's Montgomery County listed on the National Register of Historic Places.

Dayton, nicknamed Gem City, in Ohio, The Heart Of It All, in the Midwest, the Heartland of the United States—Tommy's whole life took place in The Heart Of It All: he was born in the country of Bellbrook, and bred in the suburb of Centerville.

If anyone had ever asked Tommy to describe Saint Anne's Hill he would have shared his personal perspective that provided raw exposure of his interior being, he was like that. To first shed the conversation of the obvious he would have mentioned Saint Anne's Hill's historic Victorian buildings of profound adorability, these breaths from past lives, the neighborhood overall-feeling like a soul-quivering antique store. Though Tommy admired more than history and adorability, as in they made his soul quiver but other things did too, both the lasting and the ephemeral, the profound and the not profound too. For sure he would have expanded the topic of his neighborhood by mentioning clapboard houses:

white, brown, and sky blue common colors, mint, periwinkle, and other colors also possible—he preferred uncommon colors. In life, in general, Tommy most adored the unusual, not-recommended, theoretical, and spiritual. Though, given his nature, he believed every building possessed a personality, and cherished each one in a different way.

Tommy would have mentioned dilapidated and deadbeat buildings, and he would have treasured mentioning neglected backyards littered with possibly useful junk. And he would have mentioned Gem City Catfé, diagonal from which was a mural of a lady on a balcony observing an old-time street. Oh he noticed things, heard about things, many things, and cherished plenty, but there is a tremendous difference between awareness and intimacy—Tommy was wise about only twenty or so life things in terms of practical data, mostly he was lost in his own thoughts, highly emotional, and without a desire for a life composed by mere straightforward facts.

During any of his many frequent walks around his neighborhood, the pulse of Gem City beneath his feet while on its sidewalks, also Tommy was his own set of facts, his own pulse and his own context, his own particulars and his own Gem City.

Feeling delighted living with Victor, Tommy would semi-frequently visit where Victor often was: by an open window in the sitting room, listening to his favorite type of music.

Each visit entailed listening to music, and they mainly said nothing to each other, although on occasion, to spice things up, Tommy would ask Victor, oh, "Do you like Halloween?" And through such questions Tommy would walk across the back alleys of Victor's life, for example Victor would say, "Rebecca liked Halloween," and Tommy would ask him, "Who is Rebecca?"

Though Tommy never asked Victor to explain his life, or each person in it, over time he composed a portrait of Victor: this home built by Victor's French immigrant grandfather, Gabriel, who was full of great ideas and meant for a better life just like he imagined. Gabriel founded a railroad shipping company that quickly grew; he was at the right place and time for this endeavor, like others, but others tried and he was better—many called his pizazz phenomenal.

Gabriel built himself this fine-fine, real fine home on McClain Street after his tremendous business success. His wife Simone and he shared only one son, Arthur, who continued living in the family home and taking care of the family business after his parents died. Lorraine became Arthur's wife and they had three children: Oliver, Rebecca, and Victor. Oliver, the first born, perished from this world when he was two, owing to a certain biological abnormality never fully explained to Tommy, perhaps unknown in Oliver's days, although it was difficult to know what Victor knew without mentioning.

Victor's parents also died when too young, that was what Victor would say about the deaths of both his parents and grandparents, that they "died when too young," although he never described how they died or how old they were. Victor and Rebecca inherited the business and house in a legal capacity, though only Rebecca inherited the business sense. Taking control of the business exposed her exceptional intuition that was incontestable, leading the family business into its greatest success. Victor became her assistant, and continued being her assistant after she sold the company, while it was still doing well, when she was tired and wished to retire—he was her assistant up until death visited her sleep.

There had never been another person whom Victor became close with besides his sister Rebecca, and following her death he entered a void he never before imagined. But yet while feeling truly alone, and considering himself the end of this house realistically, still his own end had not yet transpired—he posted the notecard four months after he lost Rebecca.

The home's second floor had five bedrooms: the smallest at the rear, Tommy's, with four others toward the front: Victor's, and three preserved as their departed had left them—a morbid tradition initiated after Oliver's death. Oliver's bedroom was the saddest children's room that Tommy could imagine, though all the bedrooms spooked him, Victor's parents' bedroom, the master bedroom, was as they left it when they died; same with Rebecca's.

Thankfully not only was Tommy not too bothered by feeling spooked, but in fact he enjoyed feeling spooked.

Tommy learned these facts by asking Victor questions like, "Do you prefer sunny or rainy days?" Though Victor never asked Tommy a single question, nor prompted any variety of conversation. Victor seemed fully content on not knowing a single thing about Tommy. Although now and then Tommy personally offered topics regarding his biggest curiosity: his essential meaning.

Tommy once mentioned that he truly didn't even understand why he was alive, and Victor, too old to be impressed by young dumb things, and not himself in need of approval, feeling motivated to exhibit a sharp perspective that might push Tommy in a direction where they each felt that Tommy should head, Victor replied with his own viewpoint, "You're confused, and if other people say they understand you, it's because they're confused too. Your spiritual quest is headed nowhere: you don't have an essential meaning. You won't find what you don't have, it's that simple. Your whole operation is corrupt, and when you're gone from this planet it'll be like you were never on it."

Said the man who lived in a house with bedrooms occupied by the dead. What things people say! Victor was acting as if unfamiliar with strange life currents, and speaking in a manner that some referred to as harsh reality, some called pedagogic, but Tommy considered it bologna lacking characteristics of the essential related to the imagination, and what Tommy did was nod at Victor, who was Herr Settembrini speaking to Hans Castorp in a Swiss Alp sanatorium.

Anyway on a Monday night when Tommy intended to write, instead he became consumed by introspection—the way planetary movements shine against the dome-shaped projection screen of a planetarium, so did the story of Tommy's whole life begin to shine against his skull—and thus he began feeling despondent, desiring to escape himself on account of some parts of his life really tripping him out, he decided to enter the sitting room then, knowing Victor would be there, which he was: on a grey elegantly upholstered wing chair, gazing at a window reflecting the light of a baby blue lamp on a mahogany end table next to a globe. And on the end table was a white mug certainly filled with orange juice.

Hearing footsteps, Victor turned toward Tommy without conveying a feeling, just observing Tommy before turning his eyes back to the window, this whole while listening to music that Tommy couldn't yet identify.

Tommy flipped a switch that caused white Christmas lights to begin glowing along the upper edges of the front walls, this light kissing a walnut bookcase filled with leather-bound books, a white-sheet covered piano with family photos atop it, framed Norman Rockwell covers of *The Saturday Evening Post* on the walls, and a birch pier table, populated by porcelain statues of mostly horses, in front of a burgundy velvet chaise longue which Tommy reclined upon, in front of him a bare oak coffee table, with a bronze horse bust on a marble column beside him.

To Tommy, the sitting room felt like an unshaken snow globe.

There were also old and dirty magazines and newspapers along the sides of the wall, hoarder stashes, but in their own perimeter, outside the room's walking paths, and no tremendous problem. These hoarder piles had the possibility of distressing Tommy but they didn't, for he was aware of but not bothered by Victor's eccentricities, finding them relatable in fact.

Victor's eccentricities were aspects of his personality, and what rattled Tommy was when a person didn't have a personality. A housecleaner, Tabitha, came to the house on the first Monday of every month, always bringing her husband Hank along with her. They had been the housecleaners for thirty-three years, and they would clean the dust off the hoarder piles, clean the whole house, including the phantom bedrooms, cleaning the outside front patio once a season, Tommy thought they should have cleaned the front patio more often but he didn't consider it a big deal.

This night, like usual, Tommy asked Victor, "What are you listening to?"

Victor said, "Judy Garland. Oh, Judy Garland!"

Then Tommy heard about *The Harvey Girls*, a musical based on Harvey House waitresses. He heard about long-skirted, starched, black and white uniforms. Victor said, "It was Rebecca's favorite musical."

Asking Victor about the music was a good idea, every time.

Victor told him, "Wait." So Tommy waited until one song ended and another song began. Victor said, "Listen," which Tommy did, first hearing about a trip, then learning the lead character was from Ohio.

Victor nodded while facing the window.

Tommy nodded while facing Victor.

When the song ended the album ended and what then? A new album began: an original cast recording of *42nd Street*.

Tommy felt fine being alive in this room with Victor, sitting there listening to music in the night. He became so relaxed that he drifted to sleep, later opening his eyes to discover the music was off and Victor was gone. So then he rose from the far-too-comfortable couch and made his way to the black steel spiral staircase. And going up the staircase, after it was obvious, after being nothing but true, Tommy became certain that he was walking up far more stairs than usual, looking beneath himself and seeing himself no longer where he was, the house no longer beneath his body, an expansive nothingness below him.

He felt startled and looked up—get this— discovering himself floating into sheer darkness!

And he had never floated anywhere before, certainly not like this, in a material rather than metaphysical sense. Looking down again he saw not his body then, only a land of grotesque pits and nightmare chasms filled with sawed, picked bones, and opened skulls. Then came a black ocean with light reflecting off the water, and Tommy's realization that he was a blue orb of light approaching a volcano, with a full moon in the sky.

His grandmother lived on the moon, but he knew this wasn't something she would do.

He was going up a volcano then.

And while entering the volcano it began erupting; he thought he might die right then, but everything was fine.

An indispensable component of a medium population city, a medium-sized grocery store, The Kroger Co. was founded by Barney Kroger in Cincinnati, Ohio, 1883, and became the second-largest general retailer in the United States, behind Walmart, by the time Tommy was a part-time cashier at the Kroger off Wayne Avenue.

Tommy's uncle was a Kroger manager at another store, his mother had been a Kroger manager in the past, and he considered it a stellar company with a mammoth heart, his co-workers fantastic, everything and everybody around him better than him in both a professional and private sense, based on his age, overall attitude, and work performance, which dovetails into mentioning that Tommy hadn't guessed the general anxiety that comes to one while aging.

His job wasn't depressing, he was a depressive person who felt melancholic about some things, expressing bleakness some times, which wasn't part of his job duties—he was a cashier the best he could be one, not believing it was the best he could do, it was all he was doing right then—also possessing an interior strength.

Though Tommy's worries about his potential worries worried him, weighing him down and making his best efforts relate to not being down any longer, this morning he felt tired of feeling tired, tired of giving up, tired of feeling pinned down, and so before his shift began he had made the mental plan to leave his worries behind him—a splendid idea he sometimes implemented.

On his own Tommy could find himself absent of the mood to act as if each work moment was an insurmountable tragedy, even while experiencing his common human problem of not living the life he wanted, he could remember how common him and his life problems were, and choose to view his life with a perspective uncommon to him: pleasurable.

Change your perspective and your emotions change; your life changes.

And in the middle of his shift a manager noticed his positivity before approaching him. "Tommy-

Tommy, happy to see you happy-happy!" Pure social logic. A positive job atmosphere comes from positive people, and other people, especially manager types, tend to express positivity when they see positive people, just as they tend to express frustration when they see frustrated people. *People tend to notice the obvious and feel what's easy*, and feeling awful tends to cause life to feel more awful for everybody.

Today Tommy was the same person he always was but most everybody liked him better now, since today he was not part of the problem with everything. He himself did not wish for cheap and easy smiles, but today and other days he was totally into the cheap and easy smiles other people wanted, since that could make his life feel easier, sure (though he never felt this profoundly better than anybody).

Question: when a child in his Ohio family home atop a country hill, had Tommy considered himself possessed by a remarkable destiny?

One-hundred percent, as a child and as his life continued, Tommy felt excited about his thoughts and feelings guiding him where he felt himself wanting to go, even after realizing his thoughts and feelings guided him off-course in the adult world. To expand upon that last remark: the adult world hadn't agreed that Tommy possessed a remarkable destiny, and later in his life he dabbled in daydreams about who he wasn't, picturing his life path splitting when it could have but didn't, also picturing it not splitting when it shouldn't have but did—daydreaming for kicks.

Tommy would fantasize about his other possible life paths, including ones through Los Angeles, California, and Portland, Oregon—places he had once considered moving to—imagining himself experiencing life another way someplace else.

When peak daydreaming he could picture other possible lives he'd never considered and sounded remarkable: a jet pilot who transitions to Egyptology; a successful roller rink business owner who dies happy on skates when one-hundred and twenty years old, his smile smacking the floor, his dentures popping out of his mouth and everyone calling that cosmic, sobbing while saying the world lost a smile forever, the city later building a commemorative statue in the park—Tommy daydreamed upon unique lives with extravagant qualities originating from the limitless and gorgeous possibilities of life in his imagination.

In reality he was the person who made the choices he did, and while aging he calmed himself with the mantra *open destinies*. Old enough to already should have begun long term life planning by now, he hadn't, and was it too late? It sure felt like it. Though he wasn't sure about that or anything, which was a problem of his that he couldn't deal with on occasion. Unsure of everything, he didn't want to give up on himself either, since he couldn't be sure he was as doomed as he often thought he was.

Though his life's external circumstances hadn't permitted him to encounter the life changes he felt open to, and he hadn't created these changes, he found it tricky to hope for a promotion at a job he found absurd.

He had been a cashier for three years, approaching four, which tended to be his long haul in terms of job commitments. Were his days here ending? The harder question was what would happen after his days here ended.

After running out of daydreaming gas, then Tommy chose to think about being glad to have a job he knew someone needed to have—not yet replaced by robots— feeling glad this company existed and, well, knowing he needed a job to pay his bills. He thought about positive shit like this while aware that becoming a grocery store manager would be the greatest achievement here—and did he want that to be the best he could be, if not why not, who exactly did he think he could become anyway—today Tommy did not allow his heavy thoughts to sink him, choosing not to dwell on his need for a career, despite everyone he knew having suggested he should find a career—Tommy could acknowledge that he lacked a career he needed, but his path toward a prosperous future, had anyone seen it, was it near his life skill, could anyone point to it—today what he did was experience amusing reactions to his pitch-black thoughts, concentrating on the human condition of humor and not desiring to experience turmoil regarding what he wasn't doing this Tuesday afternoon while working his one job without regret or masochistic melodrama puh-lease.

Did he appreciate this day he accepted? Well, he felt better. And feelings count for something.

He only had to pay attention to his job in order to do it, and he recalled again: robots could do this. In the tradition of working class demands, what he did at work was very little, his job not requiring mental application, special qualifications, creative impulses, nor talent. Therefore his job did not require his human personality, which was all the robots couldn't have, and he didn't find it easy or feel comfortable with a job that asked for nothing of his imagination.

And even when feeling swell he didn't encounter engaging conversation with his coworkers, or form lasting connections with customers. Pleasantries, that was all. A problem was Tommy didn't know what to chat about with most of his coworkers or customers, for various reasons such as he tended not to share their interests or curiosities. His time with each customer was ephemeral by nature—each one a small detail in a full day's work, they didn't much affect his life. Tommy knew coworkers for days or months or years, but after sharing family news and minor life accomplishments they ran out of things they could think to say to each other. Today he listened to his co-worker Richard speak about his fresh tendency to spit-fire roast, feeling thrilled about cooking food this way, and saying everyone should try it. Co-worker Jasmine spoke about finding college business homework tiresome, and considering paying Raoul to do her accounting. Tommy didn't know what to say but he knew to listen. He smiled. He nodded.

He tended not to be thinking about the same kinds of things as others, or know what to say in their kind of way. He considered himself a peaceful non-cheerful person who most related to friendly non-cheerful types of people; uncommon personalities with relatable problems.

Did he have a single coworker friend? Out of ninety-seven employees he had two friends: same-age and same-perspective Omar, and like-his-mother Emily. They vibed him, while others tended to feel repulsed by his vibes, not wanting to chat about anything related to his human condition he might mention. Most people preferred to skip human condition topics, which could hurt Tommy's feelings when he it took personal, although it only happened because most people had a different life philosophy than him: it wasn't personal but philosophical, and he felt the same way about them.

About an hour before his work shift ended he almost began contemplating the veracity of the statement, "All I need is the life I have," nearly wondering whether he could accept all that he had as all that he needed, before noticing that the exploring the truth of such a statement would be fraught with dangerous complexities related to all sorts of perspectives, including hopeless resignation, which could ruin his plan of not wanting to feel fucked today, so instead Tommy chose to think about what customers were like: the majority of customers didn't broadcast judgment, since this was the Midwest, where most people considered humanity essential, and most people were not tremendous assholes like in some places, with all different types of people finding themselves capable of being all different types of pleasant; a few customers in any random day tended to be outright pleasant-as-hell top-shelf humans who emanated robust personal confidence that felt truly inspiring.

The elderly, how extraordinarily warm and friendly they can be, very, and Tommy witnessed children evolving their responses to the mysteries of being human, noticeable personalities unknown to them taking form, innocence turning into the knowing of others. Some children exhibited awe-inspiring and precocious perspectives, some appeared clueless and mystified, and they were all too young to be wrong

Tommy always felt while mentally wishing their innocence the outright best.

Shy people of all ages, those who fidgeted with their wallets, dropped their wallets, avoided eye contact and murmured, the mere idea of being around others terrifying them, Tommy related to them entirely in every capacity and they made complete sense to him. Some customers might experience parts of their worst days at the grocery store, but Tommy had been in public during some of his worst days too, so he never held the experience against anybody else. Actually it would be better for both of them if he could be helpful.

Sometimes bummer stuff did happen to Tommy at work, such as someone could make him feel pathetic, or he could do something pathetic, but not always, and not today. Today he discovered the good amid the bad, which he could do when he wasn't acting like a baby: most customers and coworkers smiled back at him, though some didn't; some others could still label him an unreliable eccentric, which Tommy understood and didn't let it bother him. No big deal; can't win everybody.

Contrary to a common nervous day of ceaseless dread, this Sunday afternoon Tommy fit himself within the social logic of human life and everything worked out fine enough—since it was so possible, and how silly when he often acted as if it wasn't.

He remembered his life could feel pleasant if he let it. And he didn't feel bored thankfully, as feeling bored never helped nobody neither. He didn't have false expectations for this average day which was quite boring actually, feeling that one can love a boring world too: that was what Tommy was doing, as he sometimes did, when open to the idea of accepting his day for what it was, including boring.

He concentrated on scanning items, waiting for payments, sometimes bagging items, sometimes sharing perfunctory pleasantries with customers, some customers not the chatting variety—he did not freak out about his reality he embraced even while not vibing it much, only sometimes sharing a laugh with a customer, not worrying about how isolated he felt while doing what a simple robot could do.

When not vibing his life still he lived, and he didn't imagine anything terrible happening while nothing terrible happened. Then leaving from his work shift with acceptance not resentment, a positive attitude up his sleeve, feeling okay but not like surprised with himself or the world, in the parking lot Tommy crossed paths with Omar, who was heading into work.

And Omar's body language conveyed general unease, signifying a personal need for conversation, and Tommy was in a perfect mood for relating to life hardships and demonstrating eager friendliness.

Victor stopped and stood still when he and Tommy intersected; Tommy stopped and stood still too.

Omar, gazing into the distance at no particular thing, with a fixed and vacant look he said, "Went to the hospital," and paused.

Tommy wondered what.

Omar said, "Because Maha [his significant other] has been feeling real sick, too sick. She's losing her sight. Tests were taken. We're expecting a call tonight. What kind of call will it be, what will we hear, we don't know.

"And our guesses haunt our thoughts."

Tommy shook his head from side to side.

Omar continued staring into the parking lot at nothing.

Omar said, "Plus my car keeps stopping while I'm driving." He gestured in his car's direction, and Tommy turned to look at it; it looked the same as always: worn, tired. Tommy turned back to Omar and made a sad face, but Omar couldn't see his face while saying, "It's stalling I guess, but it's automatic. Something is not right."

Tommy nodded and said, "'Listening to you. On your side."

Omar turned his eyes to Tommy's before looking at the ground instead. He said, "The money—"

Tommy shook his head and said, "The damn money."

And then Omar fixed his gaze up at the sky for a moment, before glancing at the ground while shaking his head, then returning to hypnotically staring out into the parking lot at nothing. With a frustrated voice Omar said, "Life problems become money problems, so money problems become life problems."

Omar wanted to look anywhere but where he should, Tommy thought, since they were sharing a conversation and Tommy was a fan of eye contact.

He knew Omar could feel better and he said, "I know how you feel."

They each fought a beast called life—that was why they were close friends: different fights with the same beast.

Omar said, "I know you know. How are you?"

Tommy didn't think it was his time to share. Nothing he could say felt as substantial as the problems Omar had mentioned; he would not burden his friend with confessions of his own weaknesses then.

He said, "Everything's cool."

There was a pause while Omar didn't believe him.

Tommy said, "I'm trying to fake it before I make it."

No one did anything.

Tommy said, "I'm sorry to hear what you told me," immediately clarifying, "I'm not sorry to hear it, I'm sorry about what it is," building toward a final dramatic line that his emotions revealed to him right then, "I'm sorry I can't fix your problems like I wish I could is what I mean."

Continuing to thousand-mile stare into the parking lot, Omar said, "I'm not sure I can keep going.."

And Tommy laughed.

His laughter returned Omar's eyes to him.

Tommy said, "That's absurd."

Omar smiled a little, just a little, but he meant it, and Tommy had had to work for that smile.

Omar said, "I could keep sharing, overshare, there's some stuff I'm leaving out: my uncle Jaime, I'll tell you later. He's dying. I have to work. See you later alligator."

Omar left a piece of himself behind while walking into the store, and Tommy said, "After a while crocodile," but quietly and while Omar was too far away to hear him by then; it wasn't imperative anyway.

Tommy wished for the call from the doctor to be not so bad, and for the car problem to turn out to be a cheap and easy fix, while knowing that not all his wishes come true, but feeling as if that didn't mean each wish wasn't worth it, as far as he could tell, since a wish not coming true was a variety of melodrama worth the risk, he felt, as it seemed far worse to experience the loss of a wish than the loss of never having made a wish at all.

Dream makers, wish makers, troubled souls, trouble makers... Tommy and Tommy's people...

Tommy traveled from work to Roscoe's apartment, just like planned.

And when there Sukie's gaze pieced Tommy's soul as always.

A hero to Tommy, seven year-old Sukie never appeared to be experiencing difficulties related to uncertainties within existence. Sukie's mother Amanda was like that too—tonight she was at work.

A white-striped orange cat, Sukie, lay in a bed atop a wicker scratching post in the living room's corner.

Tommy sat on a grey polyester sofa facing a widescreen tv.

Roscoe smoked a cigarette on a wooden chair beneath an open window.

Johnnie Frierson's album *Have You Have Been Good to Yourself* was on its first song, the title song, when Frierson sings that being good to yourself is how you can become good to others, and Tommy agreed, since the dumb things you're hard on yourself about become the dumb things you're hard on other people about.

Both Roscoe and Tommy were about to divulge feelings they masked and avoided under ordinary circumstances, intimate speculations they couldn't share among coworkers or family members, only with each other, now and then, which felt often to them, could they have casual conversations regarding personal astonishment related to general existence.

To each other their conversations felt like pleasant strolls along a sunset beach; some say misery loves company but who doesn't—some enjoy feeling miserable about other people, while the sorrows of Tommy and Roscoe related to the two or forty million reasons they considered the world awfully challenging.

After an introductory conversation pertaining the perils of comparison—they agreed they could never be anybody but who they were—then Tommy submitted an additional topic troubling his mind during his recent days, "When I was younger I believe the world could imagine itself with me, but the world doesn't do such things, or at least not for me, so I must imagine myself with the world. And does my imagination have the strength required? On my best days I believe so, on my worst days I think it's impossible, and on my okay days I think it's tough to tell."

What Roscoe then did was perform his magic friend trick of picking up on and relating to Tommy's essential theme and, having personally considered this same topic many times before, immediately he said, "Totally. I can't believe in a world that can't believe in me. What's going on is I'm trapped in a fight with myself, and that doesn't help me in my fight with the world. I have potential don't I, here I am alive and my spirit is charged, what should I do with my spiritual energy, point it in the right direction, where is that, I'm searching, and the search is tiring me as I age, my spiritual energy is draining for no good reason, and I might die before discovering how I make sense to this world."

Roscoe and Tommy could really become intimately entangled in topics regarding the general concept of normal human existence, consoling each other's troubled minds, speaking of their fall as flight. Frankly, life wasn't as complicated as they made it sound, but life was that tricky and definitely not simple. For example, the adult world was a betting world, and it isn't always the strongest and fastest who win, but they were the ones to bet on; no one bet on Tommy and Roscoe but themselves. "They tell us we're fucked; let's keep telling ourselves something else," they either once did say to each other, or would have.

Roscoe and Tommy were approximately two of one person, the same kind of human, friends since high school and filled with the same type of hope— though the world asks for more than hope and friendship. They had always guessed that life could become a nightmare, but they hadn't guessed what the nightmare might feel like.

Now they struggled for patience in a world that had given up on them.

Roscoe was a tremendous painter with his own style but he hadn't yet figured out how to penetrate the market. So he couldn't sell his paintings and his warehouse job was one in a string of jobs that didn't point toward a potential career he wanted. He considered his twenties wasteful and felt ready to give up on his life that he hadn't figured out, or renew himself in his thirties.

Good luck either way.

Best wishes.

Kisses.

His cigarette butt in the glass ashtray, Roscoe walked across the living room saying, "I want to have a positive reaction to being myself, but I struggle being myself, and life gives me anxiety, when I already have anxiety."

It could've easily been Tommy who said it, Tommy's thoughts could come from Roscoe's words, each of them possessing abundant and passionate feelings that repelled others and bound them with each other.

Turning on his Nintendo Switch, revving up their early evening play date, readying them for *Mario Kart 8 Deluxe,* Roscoe said, "Now all I want is to pay bills and take care of myself through my elderly years."

Tommy nodded in full agreement.

Roscoe sat on an orange lounge chair beside the couch and said, "I'll feel lucky if I have more to look forward to in life than vacations. But also, hell, I'll feel lucky if I have vacations."

Further considering the topic being built upon, Tommy brought up, "I never wanted to fill my living thoughts with business worries unrelated to the pure sensation of being alive. So here I am in that situation, without a business career, but not feeling sensational, and what have I learned through experience? I can't pay a landlord with metaphysics, that's definite. Conquering my inner struggles doesn't pay my bills—I can't pay a bill by saying, 'What I'm going to do is focus on my inner struggles and not freak out about money.' I have to worry about money and consider business to pay my bills, that's as basic as the adult world is once you look at it, but I can never look at that world and picture myself within it— instead what I personally do is walk around outside quiet and alone at night, feeling less afraid about life for no solid reason, which doesn't pay my bills like I'm saying.."

Next occurred a cross between a dramatic pause and gameplay concentration. While playing *Mario Kart 8 Deluxe*, Roscoe thought about what Tommy had said. Doing better with money, seeming more secure in life on account of his significant other, still Roscoe was only one inch away from financial ruin, with no promise of a career, no retirement funds, no savings, copious debt, and still he didn't have an established future, neither did Amanda, though they had each other, they had hope and it takes more than hope but hope helps, hold on to hope and always choose love —anyway Roscoe, who might in fact one day develop into a career painter, he related to Tommy's words, and eventually he thought to say, "I have the freedom to do anything but anything I can do in the adult world sounds horrifying. And they say to me: accept what you fear. They say: be like us, not like you. They say: we're dead serious. And I'm a bad listener when they speak to me like that, I don't listen to them and they don't listen to me."

Tommy said, "I would be open to meeting a version of myself with the career I can't imagine."

Then Sukie jumped on the couch and rubbed against Tommy's leg. Tommy couldn't pet Sukie because his hands were on the videogame controller but he wiggled his leg, and Sukie rubbed her cheeks against his leg until she was lying next to him, then rolling onto her back with her chin tucked into her chest, purring without being pet.

Following Roscoe winning several rounds of *Mario Kart 8 Deluxe*, then Roscoe mentioning a recent emotional epiphany that felt relevant to their conversation, "Money: it's everywhere, it's too much, it means nothing, and I don't have enough of it."

Definitely-definitely: Roscoe and Tommy mirrored each other.

It couldn't be more obvious.

"Mhm, mhm—and I don't appreciate the soulless chores it takes to get money."

They were positive about a couple things they had agreed upon as long as they'd known each other and Tommy brought up, "We've had the same conversations since we were teenagers, you know? You know. None of our frustrations are new. Here's a question: how long will we have the same frustrations?"

"Hmm. I say I learn the hard way and I do, but I keep learning the same things again and again. It could be that I'm familiar with what's hard but don't know how to learn."

"Mm, maybe."

Conversationally speaking they were surfing dark waters, often vibing with each other while conjuring personal interpretations of a bleak existence; identifying problems more than forming solutions.

Some short minutes later, in a different mood for a similar type of conversation, following a discussion on the topic of most people considering them idiots, Roscoe turned on his Xbox One and said, "The world most adults see, I don't see it. Now, that made total sense when I was a teenager, and other teenagers felt the same. It was easier then because teenagers are dreamers—barely not kids, teenagers understand each other through their dreams. But we become older and find our lives not the same as our dreams, and discover ourselves not the same as each other.

"Myself, I overthink things—it'd be better not to think about most of what I think about. Nobody needs to worry about many of my worries, and plus I desire a life composed by more than my worries." He paused. "All these thoughts are related to each other but I can't remember what I was building toward. What were we talking about?"

Tommy shrugged and said, "I don't remember but I was listening. This sounds headed toward positive. You're building to something positive maybe."

They were playing *Cuphead* by this time, and their thoughts now felt clouded except for the game, their conversational topic at an inaccessible distance from them now, even though they had just been so near it.

Roscoe said, "I was about to stitch it all together but I can't remember how."

For a moment they felt not as if playing the game or sitting together, but as if nonexistent; and they had felt like this before.

It was no biggie and Tommy's feelings then grew from new soil, inspiring him to say, "Here's the situation we're discussing: we wouldn't want to live most the lives we don't. We don't want to be most of the people we're not. Other people sometimes suggest a problem we have is being ourselves, but what most people call problems we don't."

Roscoe said, "Yup. Based on the other people I meet I'd rather be myself. And we don't like our lives either, but for reasons different than what they usually tell us: I'm saying that although I like life I don't like the *feeling* that life gives me."

Tommy said, "Zactly. I want to like my life which frustrates me."

They shared a spiritual high-five that prompted firecrackers to go off in their souls:

Boom.

Boom.

Boom.

They were releasing their foul feelings: that's a faculty of good friendships and strong communication.

In *Cuphead*, they were about to beat a level they'd already attempted around forty times, thinking they had it figured out by then, which they did, completing it on their next try, followed by feeling satisfied by their day's amount of videogame playing.

Roscoe began rolling a joint while they continued chatting. He smiled and said, "At any rate, bitterness doesn't solve anything. Staying chill and feeling calm is close to infinitely better than feeling bitter."

"Bitterness is a waste of energy."

Minutes later they ate buttered grilled cheese sandwiches Roscoe made; Tommy was being fantastically hosted. They each drank from Capri Sun pouches. Roscoe played Noname's "Yesterday," which Tommy was glad to hear and appreciated himself, since it mentions smiles achieved through fond memories. They were appreciating life and each other, along with appreciating appreciating each other, making emotional sense to each other—while the world usually labeled them misfit rubbish. Minutes after they finished their grilled cheese sandwiches they were eating Fruit Gushers and Roscoe said, "I have a growing social anxiety that I'm not interesting and no one wants to listen to me. I don't remember how to talk to people, and I feel like there's no good reason for people to listen to me. This relates to a couple other problems I have but don't want to mention now or maybe ever, as each man dies with at least one secret or two, and I'd like to die with plenty of secrets related to what bothers me about myself."

Tommy nodded and said, "I've also never been a people person and am extremely hard on myself."

And after more conversation they could each only have with the other, after chilling and suffering together, Tommy said, "Thanks for hanging."

Roscoe said, "Sure thing, jellybean. Think about your answer to this question before we see each other next: 'Would you rather be the person who invented lightspeed travel or hologram chambers?'"

And then Tommy returned home feeling too revved up by life to read or write, deciding to release his thoughts into the air by walking around outside alone, thinking about Roscoe's question but also their conversation, stopping only to purchase an apple danish and chocolate milk at the Sunoco station obviously.

Charlie was working, and Charlie was always pleasant, probably one of the most pleasant people in the entire world. Tonight Charlie said, "Hey," and later, "See ya." And Tommy missed Charlie while walking out the door.

On a Sunday night too cold and rainy for comfortable outdoor excursions, after work Tommy was in his bedroom writing the kind of book he'd write, one about his feelings. Well, editing what he had already written, which was often how he spent time writing.

He was making lapidary alterations to his memoir, *My Autobiography Is My Manifesto: Volume One*, a narrative composed of select life memories up into his early 20s—memories chosen with genuine affection, legitimate intention, and readerly and writerly biases, not dwelling on any one memory for too long, creating a liquid narrative imitative of Tommy's feelings about life feeling fluid; he felt as if his life had not occurred for him to write about it, nor did anyone write it for him, his life just happened, and so too his book about his life became just what happened: Tommy enjoyed writing his coming-of-age adult-kids book, his bildungsroman, representing the growth of his artistic personality, his künstlerroman specifically, an adult-kids coming-of-age book that was 8.5x11", the size of a magazine,

with gigantic font

and paragraphs

across pages

this.

Familiar with an established literary subgenre, still Tommy had never seen anybody write it like this, or seen himself written about either—and who would do this but him?

He had received the fourth proof and believed *My Autobiography Is My Manifesto: Volume One* would become something like he was something, something else. In fact, one of his primary intentions was making it feel irregular, since he perceived most books as too regular, and all Tommy wanted was the pulse of a person living beneath words. He considered reasonable literature burdensome to his attention and so, choosing audacity over trepidation, having encountered many regular books before, he desired to make a book that felt unusual like him— thus designing a preposterous adult-kids memoir with a dark cartoon narrative, this had been inevitable, there had been no other possibility.

A portion of his adult life became writing what described his early life, *My Autobiography Is My Manifesto: Volume One*, which became who he was in words. All this transpired because of Tommy's instincts, which informed his love of literature. Tonight he focused on tailoring his emotional sense of self as described by *My Autobiography Is My Manifesto: Volume One*, his words stemming from his feelings that came to him with ease and grace, for better and worse—he edited for coherence.

In this circumstance he was his own boss. Having heard about self-publishing in passing before, one recent day he used Google to brush up on its basics, learning that it was easy, and a vision of paradise took shape in his mind: he became his own publisher.

There were ample precedents—he discovered for example a cult-well-known self-publishing company near Dayton, ATLATL Press in Yellow Springs, with its Ohio writers C.V. Hunt and Andersen Prunty. He ordered books by each of them: *Other People's Shit* and *Squirm With Me*. And he read these books that had grown from inside its writers, while thinking of the books growing inside of him.

He decided he would rather publish himself than not publish himself, so he would publish himself for sure. As a test, he first published poems he wrote before thinking about publishing anything. He titled this book *Earlobe*, this is a poem from it—

x

when other-dimensional guests visit
to learn about humans
i won't be a distinguished detail

i'm an example of existence but
not the greatest or among the chosen
skip me and fully understand humans anyway

okay but that doesn't bother me and still
when i go missing, important or not
some of the spectrum goes missing

i'm the kind twisted, reckless
and wild, whenever possible
that's me and my kind of people

When Tommy held *Earlobe* it was a real book that he'd published himself, that felt spectacular. He experienced emotional tingles and thought Holy Rabbit.

Realizing he could publish anything, first he wanted to feel comfortable being shamelessly excessive since only the spirit matters. He wanted to be a pinch adorable and silly but mean way more than that, intending to mean lots: in other words he wanted his book to feel like more than words, and echo his expansive personality—bare minimum. So he began writing about the world opening in front of his eyes during his early days alive, imitating his personhood through his writing, allowing his book to become what it could become (like he was becoming who he could become), *My Autobiography Is My Manifesto: Volume One* came from his life experience, his words came from his readerly experience, and he wrote what he cared to write, deliberately and recklessly subverting established writing forms in order to fly into the free sky of imaginative possibility even while being aware that publishing exposed him to bird hunters—he considered himself familiar with reality, and he would prove he was a writer without anyone's permission: how Tommy could and did do things.

He liberated himself from himself while writing about himself, and this night he edited *My Autobiography Is My Manifesto: Volume One* without freaking out about anything. On occasion he would discover he left behind bad tasting existentialism that sounded loud but meant little, and feeling reasonable while later editing he cleaned up these organic messes, sometimes, other times leaving them behind, since he liked messiness to be honest—few people like mistakes but well, Tommy was an imperfect person who made mistakes, and he considered emotional particulars fascinating on paper.

One thing was: while turning his dreams into his reality, creating *My Autobiography Is My Manifesto: Volume One*, Tommy began with an intention but not a method. He wanted to break the rules while making his book, not just to break rules and be different, but for the sake of his one true faith, creative expansion, though not all his decisions were supreme—the worst quality of *My Autobiography Is My Manifesto: Volume One* was its typography: audacious would be an appropriate adjective, but not an applicable compliment, it was atrocious, a walking disaster from a conceptual perspective. It appears as if designed by an actual child, gigantic pages and gigantic font, a gigantic mess; Tommy considered the design an appropriate reflection of his independent personality, and suitable for an adult-kids book (no one would agree).

Another obstacle: had fate kissed Tommy with a drawing talent? Hell no, not even on the cheek, no handshake neither, nothing. Therefore he could not make drawings that would have been extremely helpful in the context of an adult-kids book.

A fact is the typography was a creative catastrophe from an objective perspective: the big font that seemed adventurous to Tommy was a colossal monstrosity to others, its massive diagonal paragraphs the living dead chasing you to eat your brain—for now Tommy was a complete rookie without a clue about how to create a proper book that could sit on a respectable shelf, aware that in a certain way by doing things his own way he was creating a mistake, meanwhile he felt tremendously enthusiastic about boundless possibilities that seemed magnificent: he was able to publish absolutely any type of book! His only constraints came from his imagination. Haha because his imagination was endless and his creativity fearless.

He was blowing it and feeling fine the whole while —to him it all made absolute sense and came from careful consideration—he didn't realize what its problems were, or their repercussions, until later, through social embarrassment and personal feelings of extreme disappointment. Inspired by hindsight and audience reaction, later Tommy realized that *My*

Autobiography Is My Manifesto: Volume One felt downright amateur, unfit, misguided, and troubled enough to be a waste of belief. Isn't it obvious by now, can't you see, that the structure and design of *My Autobiography Is My Manifesto: Volume One* were analogous to Tommy? Anything not zany wouldn't have felt honest and that's that. Did Tommy have problems as a writer? Absolutely. Same as he had problems as a person. Always: the pros/cons. He edited to make his prose feel worth it.

The reason Tommy never minded being human was that other animals aren't writers. That night he thought about the dream of writing while editing his book about his life that wasn't quite a dream, *My Autobiography Is My Manifesto: Volume One*, which would would end up feeling not quite right, and that would be awkward, but he had felt worse, like when he'd never written a book, and no one ever took the book's atrocity as part of its point. In the end, *My Autobiography Is My Manifesto: Volume One* would broadcast Tommy as a rank amateur and feel plain not impressive, certainly not professional, even though it was meant to be easy-peasy and breezy reading; it became a bonkers book that felt ridiculous and as if made by a sad madman who couldn't see himself for who he was—and no one appreciated that for some reason! Wow. Tommy didn't see *My Autobiography Is My Manifesto: Volume One* as the whole problem itself —he was nicer to himself than other people were (yup).

In a professional sense Tommy was a quack writer, a charlatan uninterested in an establishment that wasn't interested in him, and he could cry about this but oh no he did not—what he did was write what he would read, having lived and read enough to know what he himself wanted to read and write, making *My Autobiography Is My Manifesto: Volume One* while listening to himself, it is a book about him, without another book quite like it.

After tailoring *My Autobiography Is My Manifesto: Volume One* some more that night then, before going to sleep, he continued reading the book he had begun reading, *Epitaph of a Small Winner* by Machado de Assis.

Tommy's adolescent life coincided with the adolescent life of the internet—which felt intoxicating.

Tommy had been informed about the internet via the television. A children's news program had asked if he wanted to chat with a person in Australia, and he thought are you kidding me. His time period's update to the Transatlantic telegraph cable, all different types of people started connecting over this particular development in the concept of global citizenry, ushering in an era of fast history, with a rapidly evolving internet integrating into people's evolving lives, it was all ephemeral and bound to fade, beautiful if you look at it that way.

During Tommy's adolescence he listened to expressionistic singer-songwriter music, visiting an internet message board dedicated to this youth music scene—along with writing website album reviews. Here he befriended others who shared his interest in sensitive music, not always agreeing with others about specific musicians, but agreeing about a certain style, not everybody getting along but everybody glad to be together. Tommy departed from this message board after becoming post-adolescent, but over a decade and a half later a Floridian board member whom Tommy had remained internet friends with mentioned that some of those people, adults now, not together on a message board still, but seasoned to Slack like professionals.

Tommy returned to an internet crowd he once knew, fondly remembering some, and feeling chill about some he couldn't remember. There was one whom he remembered bitterly: a person with a sour perspective that always agitated supposedly-peaceful Tommy. And there was another person not that interested in the idea of Tommy, but overall the reunion with some of his old internet friends was spectacular at first, when the situation was fresh.

Tommy heard about a fellow in New York City falling asleep drunk on a train. Tommy learned that fellow hadn't done this in a while but used to have a real drinking problem. The sour-other criticized the drinking, while Tommy typed *Don't sweat what already happened, now you have this story—good story*. The fellow said he was thinking about drinking again that night. And a lady in New York City typed that the fellow might as well get drunk because the next day was a holiday.

Adult vibing.

The fellow didn't drink more that night, and the next day he felt recovered; he hadn't been reentering a drinking problem and indeed the drunk night on the train had been an anomaly; Tommy had always believed in him and never expressed otherwise— sometimes fuck ups that conquer boredom are worth it.

Tommy enjoyed learning personal details like what people did in their days, and how their days made them feel; this Slack community rich with such material. The Floridian who had told Tommy about this place had not discovered his adult successful self and yet persisted on a positivity of his own design—his life not much, he let it be all that he needed(!). A Canadian was like this too: he spoke of persistence through depressed thoughts, and outdoor excursions gifting escapism. An Englishman spoke of gaining body weight while aging, and beginning a plan to shed some pounds—for Tommy and others he made playlists of the music he listened to, being into lots of pleasurable music that Tommy did not already listen to, and some music that Tommy already listened to and liked. A San Diegan mother-of-three spoke of feeling lonely and frustrated, with everybody critical of her pothead chef boyfriend except Tommy (she later married him of course—three children).

Except after a while Tommy learned about the cultural topics that many of these people relished in becoming upset about at this time, and it tired him. This was during Trump's second year, when everyone was angry about Trump. Some were angry about Elon Musk existing. Kanye West was a degenerate scumbag to some people, and they mentioned this casually while considering it reality.

Having shared intimate encounters with these long-gone internet people Tommy treasured in theory, after a while he began noticing how little interest he had in feeling pissed off about cultural topics; they only dabbled in existentialism intersecting with life anecdotes. Failing to adapt to this social environment, a dispute transpired between Tommy and several others, during Tommy defending somebody, resulting in Tommy being directly insulted and leaving this Slack place behind, feeling not insulted so much as tired; he left behind a friendly goodbye letter, remaining Instagram friends with some of them.

Facebook-owned Instagram was Tommy's preferred social network, because it was only pictures and captions. His Instagram profile was private; he followed and was followed by his real-life friends, including internet friends and distant friends, their connections enduring this way, a variety of Tommy's long distance friendships laced together only by liked photos over Instagram. Tommy mostly shared city photos from his nighttime strolls, fabulous epigraphs he encountered, snippets of movies he viewed, and photos of him with friends, some photos from his past (all the new photos becoming photos of his past

—all of his present becoming the past), little personal things that reflected his current interests, with his friends tending to understand his interests.

People who could not physically see him could symbolically be with him: Tommy was a huge fan of internet culture but it didn't consume his entire being like it did other types of people. The irreality of the internet could on occasion leave him less alone with his worries and frustrations, smiles and laughs, and sense of being, but it was not as if the internet altered his physical reality—it was only an emotional dreamscape he quite enjoyed. He liked the internet but did not think that technology would save us, no, we must save ourselves, like Tommy sometimes did by going on the internet or texting a friend.

Off from work one night, Tommy received an emoji text from his friend Alexander, who now lived in Bloomington, Indiana. Alexander would send Tommy emojis to cheer him up, and it worked every time. This emoji was a caterpillar, which Tommy found adorable, replying with a squirrel. Alexander lived alone in an apartment by a university, having recently departed from being with his high school sweetheart wife of seventeen years. The divorce had been her idea, and Alexander still believed in love, but Alexander was still divorced. He was suffering, and he would text about it, and Tommy would text back; they would call each other and listen to each other speak about the frustration they were experiencing in relation to being stuck as themselves. Alexander would say I Am Crying and Tommy would say he was there for him, which he would be as much as he could be at the time.

Tommy had crossed internet paths with writers in various ways over the years, and while texting Alexander he also texted one writer who had become his friend: Lucinella out of Phoenix, Arizona.

An internet presence and published writer, Tommy and Lucinella often reflected upon the terrors that come from being alive. Tonight she texted about the anti-anxiety medication she'd been taking for the last few months, having given her an episode after flipping her brain. To feel calmer, she had discontinued taking the anti-anxiety medication. She texted about wanting to leave from the city she lived in, and wanting her long-distance relationship with an established professional artist to endure.

Using Facebook-owned WhatsApp, Tommy sent a message to an internet friend with whom he had recently reconnected, Devashish, who lived in a 1950s-era apartment in Bombay, India. They shared a romantic perspective regarding people seemingly kept alive only through the power of art, which they discovered at an internet movie message board where they had engaged in layered conversations seeking deeper meanings, now not doing that anymore so much as understanding that aspect within each other and conversationally skating over the ice for pleasure. They discussed movies and books that reflected life dimensions—at this juncture discussing William T. Vollmann as a fascinating person.

Tommy felt blessed to hear the thoughts and feelings of his distant and internet dear friends, while unsure which conversational platforms and friendships would endure.

Tommy would have said that any story was better than the story of him, all things considered.

He could often be a real jerk to himself, once saying all he did was live and die like a dog, but how wrong he could be about himself, how ridiculous, and how disrespectful to dogs—though he kept living regardless: a fighter and a romantic, they say that love conquers all but he was single, so by golly Tommy had to love himself—which took all kinds of work, like any kind of love.

Here is a book about a man who reached from darkness toward the light, with only his fingertips ever reaching; a man who didn't make sense to the world didn't make sense to a lot of people in general—he believed in romance, but romance requires more than belief; he was a cookie, The One For Him a needle in a haystack if even present; and so he remained calm during his life's lack of a lasting romance.

In his past he'd experienced amazing others who transformed how his life felt, but none of them, however great, had ever lasted, and he could never make a person like that just happen.

Had he searched over the internet?

Duh.

Exploring realms of possibility he dated over the internet's singles matching platforms, though in fact it was never more apparent to him how different he was from other people than when he went on blind dates with internet women. Beyond his youth, and often finding youth exhausting, he dated women not in school or wondering what to do with their lives any longer, but women about his age, involved with their careers. And what of their dreams remained he wondered, while they learned he didn't have a career. Some dates were with reasonable women who never had dreams unrelated to a practical reality; Tommy sounded ridiculous to them during their date which became a waste of time. They couldn't have a straight conversation with this guy who represented the problems they never chose for themselves, lost in his own thoughts and feelings; he could drive them crazy. They wanted to talk about their day, their job, sports, news, and tv, but not their sacred thoughts and feelings. They wanted to talk about what was real[ly boring], and not share idle chatter regarding interior landscapes and navel-gazing. Though sometimes they would be professional and want to chat about interior landscapes too. And in fact Tommy met those whose troubled lives outsized his own. "My father had a brain tumor removed, he's back in the hospital with another." Tommy did not wish for the person experiencing that to feel as if no one cared; he would care. What he did was listen. "My parents are my business investors, I own a boutique clothing store, my parents ask me what I'm doing to grow my business, and what can I do, I'm doing what I can do, I'm on the internet, you can shop at my store on the internet, I make enough to pay my rent, and how does them asking me what I'm doing help me?" Was she intelligent? Tommy wouldn't have said she wasn't, but she kept mentioning worrying about it. He would listen and relate to other people's fights with life, and the lower the person felt the more he was on their side. "I didn't date anybody for about two years—I didn't believe anybody would date me," he'd hear and want to let this person know he was glad they were themselves. "I'd lived in Boston but now I've moved back home with my parents; I teach GED classes but I don't know what the rest of my life will be like," Tommy related to troubled others, that's been mentioned—but a relationship takes more than relating. And also he would hear, "Sorry but you're not my type," while being there without a type in mind. He would experience women giving up on him quite fast. And he would encounter women willing to see what would happen. There he would be in a bar, buying drinks he wouldn't otherwise buy, drinking during dates for social relaxation, one or three drinks and always it would be two people wondering how to talk with each other, in order to find out what they liked about each other. Oftentimes, because Tommy would bring these topics up—"biographer questions"—they would each speak of their childhood home, and some of what they thought of life, some of how they felt about being themselves, and things they did for fun, what their interests were: general contextual information like that. But he would tire of the questions others would tire of being asked. What they each wanted to really know was if there was a spark between them. When had Tommy last seen a spark? A few years ago, and not from the internet. A spark is a thing that can't be forced; conversations can't make it happen, but if a spark is there it lights the conversation. When a spark is there it's in front of your eyes the whole time. It's fire in the void. And a spark is so rare that some women wouldn't be considering it even, wise enough to be aware of its rarity. Tommy thought that was a mature perspective, an objective perspective, which he learned about from women. The night could be a simple escape from loneliness, nothing more and nothing less, if it went all right—if each person was operating on automatic, in terms of being nice to each other, and liking being around each other—how simple. His internet dates were often a one date experience, sometimes abbreviated, "TMI but I have a bladder infection," suddenly, though sometimes the date would stretch into the night, sometimes with a goodnight kiss, sometimes many kisses and his shirt collar being clutched. Sometimes there would be a second date, as if maybe. Sometimes a few dates. But often only one. The longest internet relationship Tommy experienced? His second longest was one that lasted for a week, although they tried their luck twice, for a total relationship runtime of a week and two days. She ended them first; he second. He had been broken and done the breaking. Other times he had been ghosted and done the ghosting. How very apparent it was to him, and them, that Tommy was not meant for many types of women. Some felt clueless about how to be themselves, and Tommy could relate, but he could not wait. Some felt afraid about who they were, and he would be on their side, but it was going to be a long fight, and it was another man they needed. He had been given up on and done the giving up. He had thought, "You are not The One," and wondered "How was I not The One?" Here was the foulest: when there was no reason to not want to be with her, but he could not want to be with her. He could not always define what was happening. Who completes you completes you, and nature cannot be reduced to comprehension. What did he most desire from a woman he dated? He wanted to be with someone who wanted to be with him in a spiritual capacity, believing in the power of herself and him, their combined powers elevating them above the frozen land of reality; a tale of romance. Not making promises he would not keep, Tommy would not make promises to these women; not falling in love, he would not say he was in love with them. On occasion during dates he would reference life feeling terrible, but one does not go into full detail about such things while casual dating, although if they went into it themselves he would most certainly listen. All Tommy knew was his biggest internet dating problem, the main problem, was there was never a spark. He would go on internet dates when feeling alone, but after a while preferring to feel alone again; not because loneliness was healthier, but because it made more sense: being alone felt better from a practical perspective, based on his internet dating experiences. A summary of his dating life: nighttime dates to nearby bars, with women he did not know traveling to and leaving him. And in his mornings he would wake and wonder why he was awake, missing being asleep. Anyway the answer to the question about the longest internet relationship was two months. From October to December he dated a divorced woman whose husband-since-high-school had left her because he didn't want to have sex with her anymore. Her and Tommy dated a year after the divorce—she was very, very into sex. She had become a sex fanatic after her divorce—and was that not understandable? Tommy had sex with her. She would wear lingerie, methodically squirt, and was open to anything. And they enjoyed hanging out with each other. She was nice. But there wasn't a spark. So he told her, once he was certain. He said he told her to be honest with her, having once experienced a woman tell him this. Tommy did not like being on either side of this. How rotten it feels to be a part of the world's sadness. He longed to be more than what was sad. Maybe become friends with her? He clarified that he liked her as a person and liked hanging out with her, and liked having sex with her, but maybe they could hang out without sex. She agreed. Then they had sex. Then he saw her again and they had sex. Then he saw her again and they had sex. And he didn't know what to tell her then. She said she felt as if he was slipping away. It was because he was slipping away.

Why could he not be there for this woman who wanted to be loved and fucked?

Didn't he want to love and fuck?

He wanted to love and fuck, but more than that he wanted a spark to bring fire to the void.

So he himself indeed contributed to life's persistent sadness.

While pleasure rereading the first chapter of Anton Chekhov's *My Life,* Tommy's mother called him.

Then some minutes later he was formatting the latest draft of his mother's recent memoir, *Hellhole,* which depicted her interior strength allowing her to endure the bad sides of the life she witnessed as an assistant to a Hollywood notable.

Part of the reason his mother wrote was to inspire Tommy as a writer, she said, but she would also say that writing was in her blood. Tommy inherited his desire to write his personal perspective from his maternal side—only they believing that writing was in their blood. His mother's first book had been *One Little Black Book,* which had been about her childhood, and she was finishing her second book, *Hellhole,* which was about a couple years ago. His mother had moved to Southern California to live near her daughter, Tommy's older half-sister, who lived in Newport Beach with her husband and their four children. Previously his mother had changed her mind about *Hellhole*'s font size and, through feedback and time, made a number of small edits, this therefore being Tommy's third time formatting *Hellhole*. He found this formatting experience less frustrating than the previous two because he was used to the whole operation now, and this was for his mother, so he felt reminded that he needn't feel frustrated while doing any little thing, being certain that assisting his mother was related to his essential meaning for sure.

He formatted *Hellhole*, set it to the lowest possible price (ninety-nine cents), and submitted it for a publishing review.

Doing the things his mother asked him to do—not at all feeling as if wasting his life's time.

Then he called her to say he was done, and some other things related to what she had asked him to do. "I can't set the number of preview pages. That's something set by the site."

Innocent, she replied, "I earn money when someone looks at the preview pages."

"You don't."

"I can't hear you, you're breaking up."

"You can't hear me at all?"

There was a pause before she hung up.

He waited to see if she'd call back.

After she hadn't called back he went outside for better reception.

That was a good idea because when he called her again she said, "I can hear you better now."

So he repeated what he'd said.

And after his mother realized she'd only make money from ebook and physical book sales, not from people reading preview pages, then she began explaining that she wanted her book to enter the top ten sales chart, in order to receive a twenty-five thousand dollar bonus.

Her voice was filled with passionate conviction while she told him this. Tommy was there for his mother, but also what she said scared him. He said, "I'm excited for you. I'm glad to hear you—your strength, your determination, your unwavering personal conviction and the way you've taken care of yourself through your life has inspired me. We're older now and everything, we're both older, and I just want to mention that we know nothing is promised. Being in the top ten is hard, pretty rare."

His mother told him she read about a lady who wrote a parenting book that made it into the top ten. She said if that lady could do it she could too. "That's why I set my book to its lowest price. To encourage more people to buy it. I won't make money off the sales, but I only make a little money off the sales, and I'll make more money on the sales chart. And I have a whole group of people helping me." She mentioned that being anywhere in the top one hundred sales meant money bonuses; less money in lower spots, still some money. She mentioned that her three sisters and brother were spreading the word, and she mentioned that the author of the parenting book had sent out emails, so she had hired two online advertising firms to send out emails—one from Italy and one from India.

Tommy, delighted by and worried about her level of excitement, said, "Good, good. I think you're doing what you can do. But we're older, and I just want to say that this is what you're trying now, this is your plan this month, and I'm glad you already have a plan for the future." His mother's other plan was to work in a new coffee truck with her housemate. Part of the reason she wanted to win money was to help finance and co-own the coffee truck. Tommy said, "I'm proud of you, you always find your own way through this world. You always have more than one plan."

She said, "Is there anything I'm not seeing? I edited my book. This one I edited myself, since with my last two books I learned about how the editors change your voice. I used three editing programs: Word, Grammarly, and this one I found, the Hemingway Editor. I put my writing through those three."

He said, "That's great, that's really great."

A mother speaking to her son, a mother speaking to someone who would never be against her, again she asked, in a quiet voice, a vulnerable voice, a trusting voice: "Is there anything I'm not seeing?" And her question rattled Tommy's sense of being, sending chills up the spine of his essential meaning. Tommy and his mother were in a situation that he couldn't solve for her. He wanted for her what she wanted for herself, but he couldn't give it to her. What she could do differently he didn't know better than she did. He didn't believe he saw more of the world than his mother did. He didn't feel that he knew the world better than she did. He said, "Neither of us know what will happen. I don't know what books everyone will read. I have different perspectives about this world than most people, and I felt the same as you when I released *Earlobe*. I worried about everything. I tried to take care of what was necessary. But how do I know what's necessary? And so much comes from how people react—and people react not how I want them to, but how they do."

There was a pause where for one brief moment Tommy wished he had said just the right thing that would've solved everything.

He said, "I think you're believing in yourself and that's a right thing to do, an important part of what's necessary."

She said, "What I've heard is things don't happen to people who give up."

He said, "I've heard that too. It sure doesn't help."

She said, "I don't want to give up on this. There's a thing…"

He noticed, "Do you want to tell me a story?"

She said, "Yeah, it's an important one. I once went to an art show with my friend, and when entering we saw an amethyst sculpture that was a raffle prize. I said, 'I'm going to win that statue.' My friend laughed and said, 'Everyone thinks they'll be the winner.' Then later the prizes were being given out. The first thirty prizes were given out. The amethyst sculpture was last. And I stood up before my name was called. I knew it'd be me. I *knew*. And it was. That kind of feeling has only happened to me one other time in my life, when I won money to buy your first computer. I want that feeling again."

She said, "That kind of confidence."

Again and again through this entire conversation, Tommy wanted everything his mother wanted to happen to her to happen to her. He wanted that so badly. And still he couldn't place his mother's book on the top one hundred sales chart. He wanted her book there with all his heart but he couldn't just put it there. Did he think her book deserved it? Now it's been mentioned thrice: he thought his mother deserved everything she wanted and more.

All he could do wasn't enough in a practical sense, but in an emotional sense he did what he could do, which was love her; if he'd ever be on someone else's team he'd be on his mother's.

Later that night his emotions began sinking in quicksand although he wasn't aware of this, even if he might have guessed. Snow made the city a blank page and Victor sat on the grey elegantly upholstered wing chair by the open window, and *Pickwick* played from speakers, "If I Ruled the World," while Tommy read "Sailing to Byzantium" on the burgundy velvet chaise longue.

Tommy looked at Victor: what did Victor mean to anybody? There was Victor and he meant a great deal to Tommy.

The adult world bored Tommy, as it bores any person with even an ounce of the wild in them, so leaving Kroger after a NYE closing shift he said two things: Goodbye Forever, and See You Thursday.

Then it was a quiet first day in a new year that felt the same as all the rest; Tommy couldn't spot the difference. It wouldn't have surprised or bothered him if he heard the new year was only a rumor. Alone and unafraid, he didn't think much about this morning or life at all, since the situation didn't demand it and he wasn't in the mood; and minutes passed, minutes passed, but no worries traveled with them, until too many minutes passed and the concept of time reasserted itself, instigating regret about time lost: how little he had accomplished in a day that was one of his mortal few. Didn't he wish to accomplish things while being alive? This alarming question gifted him the motivation necessary to rise and go to the bathroom across the hall, where through an open window he heard a car s*woosh*. Then he was back on his futon and prepared to make a decision about what to do on a new day in a new year, listening to mood-setting decision-making music, Randy Newman's "Dayton, Ohio - 1903."

He began his year by pleasure reading Charles Baudelaire. Because one goes where one is called. And reading Baudelaire filled Tommy's thoughts with topics related to the power of life and writing, so much so that his thoughts came to feel overflowing, interrupting his reading and causing him to venture outside to stretch his thoughts without walls or ceilings.

Thus began this day that turned to night, and during day and night the Earth revolves the same, but others don't know what to do without the life-giving sun, and the sun gave Tommy life too, but he dreamed at night beneath the sleeping eyes of a business world, with his dream energy arriving from the moon. His walking route this night, not symbolic, but cosmic, was shaped like a helmet if traced on a map: McLain Street to High Street, onto Plocher, Mcreynold, Josie, and up an alley back to McClain. He wore a black sweater over a black t-shirt, with black boots and black socks, black jeans and black undies. Black fingernail polish.

The wind tickled his clothes, licked his face, and made the tree leaves dance under street lamps. The streets smelled like a sweaty vampire and the cars said *whoosh, swoosh-whir.* He waved to his grandmother on a waxing gibbous moon while a red-haired bearded man, carrying an orange cat, passed by on an apple-green bicycle.

Walking beneath the immensity of the night sky, able to think about whatever he wanted to think about, this night he wrote a Post-it note he left himself on the refrigerator in his mental kitchen:

Die Dreaming

He left this note next to many notes, and a postcard from Spain, some notes the same, only one postcard from Spain.

Tommy strolled his neighborhood alive with his own perspective, noticing what he did, thinking what he thought, being who he was, and that was how things were. Who he felt meant to be was himself, this hadn't been his choice and was already true. What he tried to do was not become disappointed in a world that could become disappointed in him, loving himself in a tough world. This was his life, and his whole life felt absurd and outrageous the entire while: his essential meaning's best bet was the butterfly effect. That was fine. He could handle that by thinking about how he had to. Because if he had to then he could.

And he reflected on his yesterday that was already over, what it had been like, what it could have been like, who he was, who he could be, and what his tomorrow might be. Standard Tommy in his real life: curiously and anxiously onward, with mild excitement.

His three life hobbies: reading, writing, and walking around, which he performed while searching for, escaping from, and experiencing his essential meaning. He was a common human variety and yet, owing to complexities in a massive universe, and universal possibilities within human existence, it was often challenging for him to encounter other people who desired to same-level engage in abundant curiosity from beyond innocence, most often encountering similar people by reading. Out in reality, where were the others whose thoughts danced with their dreams? They were the ones both everywhere and tough to find, Tommy knew like three of them.

One step after another, each step his own, he strolled the sidewalks of Saint Anne's Hill with a life composed by more than facts—and building from these parameters, considering these ideas and other ideological components not being mentioned but you can imagine, in response to all of this inside of Tommy's head and heart, some of his best walking came from wondering nothing.

Wandering around wondering zilch allowed his thoughts to vacation outside the dwelling place of his rabbit hole of introspection. During the majority of his adult life he operated under a troubled perspective regarding general existence, so he relished when he could find the space and time to take an existential vacation, and that night he brought himself where he always enjoyed arriving: feeling mellow wondering nada, only noticing oak tree leaves shimmy in the wind.

Real talk: he was more into feeling mellow than feeling anxious. Though while thinking about diddly-squat well anyway soon a topic of immense importance would occur to him, prompting immediate consideration, one important consideration often instigating another, pushing him further and further away from free and easy nothing. This night while walking around thinking about nothing for a little while, he then began remembering this whole thing that is going to go ahead and be omitted from the record.

Regardless: Tommy would be in the city and the city would be in him; the city would be in front of his eyes and behind them. His neighborhood sidewalks were never anything but themselves, same as him. This night he cruised the sidewalks like he meant it, which he did, it was his walking style.

The sole location where Tommy treasured walking equal to his neighborhood was near his work: Woodland Cemetery, one of the oldest garden cemeteries in the United States. He often strolled there directly after leaving work during their regular open hours though also, when feeling devilish and seeking patterns beneath the shadows, if let out late enough for the neighborhood to be asleep after Tommy worked a closing shift, and especially if there was a full moon, when feeling summoned by these sacred grounds what Tommy did was sneak across the fence and engage in secret nighttime cemetery strolls that gifted him tremendous personal satisfaction which would've been difficult to explain if he was ever busted, though he never was, no one noticed, no one cared—sounds like Tommy.

People with graves at Woodland Cemetery: the pioneers of aviation; the famous poet who spoke of the caged bird singing; the inventor of the folding stepladder; the inventor of the cash register; the pioneer of the Yellow Pages; the father of American beekeeping; a lawyer who shot and killed himself while proving to a jury how a man could shoot himself while drawing his gun, the defendant cleared and released; a child's grave often decorated with gifts left for him and the dog who pulled his drowned body from the river, the dog having stayed by the boy's grave until he died too; a twenty-nine thousand pound boulder commemorating a humorist and syndicated columnist; and in the cemetery's middle a twenty-foot column surmounted by an angel in white marble, dedicated to the Stanley clan, who had a vault made of stone slabs too, with more than fifty clan members buried at Woodland Cemetery, including three Kings and two Queens of the Gypsies.

In addition: Lookout Tower, the highest point in the city of Dayton.

And a chapel with a Tiffany stained glass window.

A cemetery with a strong personality.

A fabulous cemetery as far as those things go.

Tommy's Thursday, after a closing shift, there was a full moon, he waved to his grandmother, and guided by voices he strolled along Goose Lake Road in Woodland Cemetery, as he often did, a favorite spot of his. At first alone but for history and the wind, everything was normal while he walked in darkness. On his mind at this exact time who knows, some topics more possible than others, anyway this night he saw them out there on Goose Lake, he was sure, there they were, right in front of him, licked by moonlight: thirteen ghosts on nine ghost boats. And he felt excited then, beginning to careful-quiet walk toward Goose Lake while unable to recognize any of the ghosts, and not knowing a damn thing about boats. He sat on the grass, beginning to notice the obvious: the ghosts were dressed 19th century, and their wooden boats had ornate designs.

At first he stared and felt stunned, shivered some.

Then he realized the ghosts were talking.

He about did a backflip when he realized that.

He began listening, overhearing one ghost say to another, amid quiet sobbing, "I absolutely…terribly miss Christina." And Tommy highly suspected that the ghost would never see Christina again, no matter how badly he missed her. In fact, Tommy considered it certain that Christina was gone forever. Tommy felt the vibe and detected an eternal harmony between himself and the ghosts, sixth sensed it, immediately craving to learn about these phantoms alive to him, and prepared to experience acute empathy.

This whole experience felt spectacular, with some absolute stand-out moments—all of this no-doubt a product of his grandmother's design. At one point one ghost alone on a boat sang a remarkable song of tremendous beauty, with the vocal range of a true professional, a deep bass that was honey in Tommy's ears, and other ghosts turned to smile while they too heard:

> Beautiful dreamer, wake unto me,
> Starlight and dewdrops are awaiting thee;
> Sounds of the rude world, heard in the day,
> Lull'd by the moonlight have all passed away!
>
> Beautiful dreamer, queen of my song,
> List while I woo thee with soft melody;
> Gone are the cares of life's busy throng,
> Beautiful dreamer, awake unto me!

The whole while: the ghosts' facial expressions fascinated Tommy. One woman alone on a boat had a face that appeared more stern and scared than any other: stern when another ghost glanced her way, scared when none did—she was the ghost Tommy related to the most, though he appreciated them all.

A side fact: Tommy entered the cemetery feeling bad that night, not from entering the cemetery of course, but from having experienced what he felt was a low day for reasons related to particular circumstances being omitted right now, similar ones described elsewhere in the book. Something being omitted had rattled his sense of essential meaning earlier that day, but Tommy began thinking about the ghosts on boats more than himself, allowing his thoughts to settle in a place outside himself.

Tommy heard a child proclaim, "I was not born in the wrong time, I was born in the wrong family." The two adults with her, clearly her parents, appeared dumbfounded: the child had sounded one-hundred percent like she meant every word. The child turned her eyes away from her parents, and Tommy slapped his knee. The parents discontinued their frustrated whispering and the boat entered a silence dense with dreadful tension—she had said what she wanted to say, the adults didn't know how to respond, no one knew what to do, and Tommy slapped his knee again.

The ghosts had nowhere else they wanted to be, and neither did Tommy. He adored them, perhaps loved them, so much so that he yelled, "I can't wait to be with you!"

For several minutes he wondered if he'd even have a ghost boat one day.

Then very late that night, right before dawn, after *by accident* he nodded off for *one second,* perhaps momentarily overdosing on bliss, then he opened his eyes to see what he adored having vanished, absolutely wishing the ghosts had disappeared by melting into the sky at dawn as he had guessed they would.

He reacted by howling at the moonset black sky and crying quiet tears while leaving. And the phantom boats didn't show up on Goose Lake the next night, when he brought two friends along, nor other late-nights when he visited alone again; not even other full moon nights when he wished aloud, Please Grandmother, Once More. Though Tommy wasn't bothered by his one night with the ghosts of course, as mysterious nights were his favorite sort, along with his favorite types of people being those coming from and heading toward places he couldn't guess. He continued feeling as if making solid life choices and spending time wisely while strolling Woodland Cemetery, and his neighborhood of St. Anne's Hill, where history lived, and he overall felt like this: Dayton was a historic city with its best days behind it, proud of its past, a tired city now, gone to bed but not yet asleep, still some thoughts in its mind.

Tommy hadn't seen his old-friend Jake in over a year, and he considered that a sad fact, although this was a personal opinion he hadn't mentioned to anybody.

But synchronically, one early afternoon when Tommy was off from work and lying on his navy blue futon wanting to ponder his life, but finding his life imponderable, and thus feeling unable to decide what even to do with himself, about to begin deliberating if he was doomed or not—Jake texted him from out of the blue:

> Hey
> Where should I buy a hat?

And about twenty minutes later they were both inside a hat store with all manner of hats except for baseball.

Tommy first spotted Jake considering a yellow safari hat with tender analytics.

Following which, Jake, a rock climber, amateur photographer, lead designer in a sign store, and born/bred country boy, pointed to a grey gambler straw hat he placed on his head and said, "Grey is my color. I'm a grey person. Some people are brighter colors, such as," and he pointed to the yellow safari hat he had returned to the shelf, "I dig—no, okay, I love—that humongous brim, and that hat's lightness—but myself, as a person, I can't fulfill the promises of being yellow. Some days I'm not bright yellow. Yellow expresses joy. Some heavy days I'm not very joyful is what I'm saying. Some days that light-bright hat wouldn't be right for me, but I'm always ready to be grey. I can be grey anytime; I usually am. You remember what grey is? Overcast: not quite dark; aware of darkness but not consumed by it; near darkness but don't exaggerate—that's me."

Tommy smiled, nodded, felt it: totally.

Tommy wore a black leather jacket over a black t-shirt, with black jeans, black socks and yellow sneakers.

Jake appeared partially insane weather-wise since it was a cold day and he was in an orange t-shirt, electric purple shorts, slime-green socks and dry-mud brown sandals; he was the kind of guy who pushed the boundaries of reason in country ways that Tommy considered understandable, adorable, and traditional Midwestern. Jake wasn't the least bit concerned about other people's tastes or what would be considered a good idea, not ignoring these things but never being bothered by them in the first place.

Neither Jake nor Tommy believed that it mattered much if anyone was wrong about everything they did throughout their entire lives regardless—only their spirit mattered.

Guided by voices, Jake bought the grey gambler straw hat. And he wore that hat while driving his muddy black pickup truck toward a place they had enjoyed visiting many (three or four) times since they were teenagers, his and Tommy's favorite small nothing creek off the road in the middle of nowhere.

Jake had once taught Tommy how to cast a fly rod, but it wasn't Tommy's art. Incredible: through time and dedication, talent and commitment, Jake had developed a casting ability that expressed his inner nature, yup, his true self glowed while he cast a fishing line off a fly rod. That day, lickety-split and beautifully, transcendentally, Jake caught a small bluegill he returned to the creek. And soon after that he caught a small crappie, which he returned to the creek as well.

Jake said, "This is the real world, Tommy. Nature. Nature is the real world, and here are the surprises of life that don't cost a cent."

Absolutely nothing was going on in Tommy's mind at this time; how he felt was incredibly refreshed by nature. All his life's terrors couldn't see him here; they waited back in society. He smiled while the wind whispered fresh dreams, and nature felt generally erotic. In fact his soul felt turned on during chilly overcast conditions, with weeds and wild grass quivering beneath him.

Then Jake and Tommy were back on the road, with the truck's heat on and its windows down. Acting free and wild, Jake drove up a hill and into the clouds;

Woohoo Tommy felt but didn't yell even though he authentically could have. What was up in those clouds? Memories of other times they'd traveled across these roads like this: sweet.

Raised nostalgic for the past and future (Ohioans), Jake and Tommy each felt as if not belonging to the time they lived inside, wanting to live on this same planet during any other time, and neither of them had a shopping agenda or felt as if in a hurry while heading to antique stores in downtown Waynesville.

The inevitable transpired: sauntering three neighboring antique stores, they practiced modes of perception upon immensely charming and utterly human wares embodying reflections upon past lives and possibilities, both satisfying the needs of their now and gifting Tommy and Jake sublime perspectives outside their own.

While experiencing emotional traction during their antique stores excursion, Tommy developed a nagging curiosity regarding what his favorite color might be, initially guessing it was probably dark purple. Though eventually he noticed a certain sunflower-patterned depression glass piece colored plum purple, thus concluding plum purple was a more accurate answer.

Jake and Tommy each felt downright blissed-out while in the country admiring household anthropology: free from worries or regrets or anything like that, no reason for those things right then.

They returned to Dayton during a magnificent sunset, followed by stained hardwood floors and brick walls, dangling plants, a vaulted wooden ceiling, skylight windows, a balcony section, and their round wooden table with two glasses of water.

Jake and Tommy treated themselves to a Thai and sushi restaurant in Oregon District. Thai 9: what was it like that night? A regular waitress without a wedding ring was there, the one whom Tommy developed a crush on after first meeting, thinking perhaps a natural magnetism had occurred between them, since she appeared to like seeing him as much as he did her. He watched her eyes as she smiled at him during their initial mystery period, although quite quickly she discontinued her mysterious smiles. She had solved the mystery herself. Tommy noticed and discontinued wondering how she felt about him, since he understood the roulette of romance, still now-and-then visiting here for food, and continuing to smile at her, but with less vibrant smiles now, since he didn't want to ruin his smile's reputation for wholesome sincerity, following everything that never existed between them being already over.

Mostly the restaurant was populated by other thirty-somethings, although next to Jake and Tommy were three teenagers dressed in sharp new clothes that Tommy would have to Google. Tommy noticed their sneakers had straps covering their laces. Stylistically, teenagers may have revolted against the aesthetics of laces: imaginable since fuck everything.

Tommy had felt like a teenager when he was one, but now he wasn't so he didn't. The teenagers were who he no longer was. They looked sharp, in fact better than he had, but still they were unaware of how unaware of life they were; Tommy sat there eating drunken noodles and thinking about this while also reflecting upon life experience having taught him that today's smiles don't make promises for tomorrow, and more than smiles take place in life, which can be frightening, but also more than happiness is necessary, and more than innocence is beautiful; Tommy found maturity sexy, and his favorite type of person was a person recovered from feeling broken.

And by consequence of these contemplations he mentioned these topics to his dear friend Jake, whom he considered a superb listener.

Jake said, "What the hell? Just plain live for fuck's sake."

Tommy said, "Well, anxiety sneaks into my thoughts like teenagers sneak into parks at night."

It was a delightful-enough meal in a neat-enough restaurant after a fine-enough day with a chill-enough country friend. It didn't cure Tommy's existential worries but he hadn't thought it might; it was only a vacation from such.

Following dinner, Tommy and Jake walked across the street to Bonnett's Book Store; Tommy's idea.

Tommy's special order of Marguerite Yourcenar's *Memoirs of Hadrian* had arrived. He bought that and, since he noticed it right there, there it was, he bought it, *Zami: A New Spelling of My Name* by Audre Lorde. Plus, after considering it a golden opportunity, responding to his emotional necessities, and mentally organizing his food finances (remembering an excellent four dollar combo at Wendy's), he ended up buying an affordable used copy of Grace Paley's *The Selected Stories* too.

Then Tommy told Jake he'd walk back home alone, since he was the type of guy who would do that. They told each other, "Goodnight, good luck," and really meant it. Following which, Tommy strolled his neighborhood sidewalks feeling fortunate carrying books.

Then it was another day and Tommy's tiny life implied his world was tiny but yet abundant life surrounded him: he was contacted by another old friend, this time Ronny, a computer programmer at LexisNexis who made gobs of money compared to Tommy—though Ronny was still paying off enormous school loans, debt from prior alcohol and gambling addictions, mortgage on a newly purchased suburban home, and two car payments, plus providing for the daily needs of his significant other and their three children, alongside continuing to search for his true and full self—Ronny had created a YouTube exercise series that lasted one episode (Tommy had begged for the second that never arrived), designed an app that recorded practice time sessions for guitar players, founded a company to sell the app, wrote and self-published a book about financial investment, and sold retail items on the Amazon marketplace—searching for what might fill him while accomplishing what didn't.

Despite understanding life being hard, it didn't overwhelm non-outrageous Ronny, who reminded Tommy about guy stuff: accepting the world for what it was, and himself for who he was. Ronny was a solid plan maker with a practical perspective instead of a living manifestation of his perpetual fight with life;

dull melodrama. Turned out acting non-outrageous had its pros and cons like everything, since still Ronny couldn't get from life what satisfied him, and he was missing out on sensational melodrama.

But Ronny related to Tommy at an elemental level, which was mutual, as Tommy related to Ronny's relentless quest for his true and full self. Tommy felt optimistic about Ronny's future and, personally, looked forward to living in Ronny's home after the kids moved out. Ronny was his three-year old son Joel's biological father, loving Joel in a fatherly way of tremendous and sincere proportions; Tommy could just tell that Ronny would be a terrific father who throughout his entire life would be on Joel's side every time—it was plain obvious. Ronny's other two children were his seven and nine year-old step-daughters, whom he had known since they were three and five: Ronny grew up with his children.

Friends since high-school, Ronny and Tommy knew a lot about each other, not everything but more than most. Often Tommy felt accepted being himself around Ronny, as in Tommy could commit blunders and be minor outrageous without Ronny holding it against him, though Ronny could act slightly irritated now and then, that was okay, could just maybe happen, understandable. Despite in fact being so different from Tommy, and without sharing anywhere near the same types of particular life problems, nor cultural interests, literally nothing in common, not a single thing, still, Ronny and Tommy related to each other as companions in miscellaneous idiosyncratic misfortunes, each of them considering reality rude, and with Ronny himself experiencing strange moods on occasion.

Their years of friendship had taught them they could feel comfortable around each other, and one winter afternoon they met to have lunch as they sometimes did—this time Ronny offering to pay, so during his lunch break they could meet at Scramblers, each ordering breakfast food: Tommy a Zesty Smokehouse, Ronny a Wisconsin Scrambled.

They each treasured restaurants with abundant calmness as an interior design; casual atmospheres evoking nothing but soothing calmness. It looked to Tommy as if people could eat here and there wasn't much more to mention really; he evaluated how human the place felt. This place felt perfectly human and not much more: excellent. Ronny and Tommy were not into too-nice places fishing for compliments, since Ronny and Tommy felt most comfortable when not exerting concentration toward appreciating anything that made happiness seem to require extra effort—Ronny and Tommy thought Scramblers looked fine and everything was all right in terms of personally treasuring Midwestern aesthetics.

Speaking from a mellow place Ronny said, "I took out a loan as a hedge against inflation. Specifically at seven percent over five years. I'm consolidating my nine percent debt, which is freeing up some capital to trade. My current plan is to buy and hold some commodities while selling covered calls on a fraction of the days they spike. I think I can beat my fixed interest rate. If not, I can simply return the money. No origination fee, no early payment fees.

"I'm mostly worried that China might not be buying treasuries anymore."

None of that had anything to do with Tommy's life, but he listened because Ronny would listen to him.

Ronny said, "Also I read China isn't accepting a lot of US recycling anymore, but that's another issue."

There was no real reason for them to be interested in each other, and yet they bonded beyond reason, by human nature, their friendship yet another fine example of human nature's capability of being more beautiful than reason. After their food arrived Tommy, considering the doozy life story of Gilles de Rais an unusual variety that packs a wallop, and having read about it recently, thinking Ronny might want to hear about it, he began speaking about the companion to Joan of Arc who became a serial killer of boys, mentioning that Gilles de Rais [pronouncing the name Gee day Rah] did things like sit and smile on boys while they died.

Tommy concluded by mentioning, "And—part of the reason he sacrificed boys was to summon the demon Barren."

Then he became quiet for a dramatic effect that didn't give Ronny any facial expression at all.

Ronny said, "Well, I read just the other day, you see, Gilles de Rais [pronouncing the name Zheel duh Ray] was innocent, never a serial killer or occultist, his trial part of the Inquisition, he was forced into losing by his prosecutor the Duke of Brittany, who'd receive his land once he died."

Tommy felt shook. "I'm hearing some facts. You read this just the other day?"

"Yeah. The writer said it's a story people read without looking into—an often repeated story full of dust and moonlight."

"Dust and moonlight, pretty."

Ronny made a face that expressed not thinking Tommy was following along.

Feeling as if he tripped over a conversational pothole, Tommy said, "I'm hearing reasons it's a five hundred year-old story. I think it's fascinating."

Ronny said, "You think of this as *fascinating*?"

Tommy hadn't been prepared to defend the probable innocence of Gilles de Rais, despite having scanned the Wikipedia section about the topic, not quite expecting absolute truth from old court rooms anyway, especially concerning boy-killing demon-worshippers, anyway Tommy's integrity felt twisted and he felt defensive about seeming for a second as if a disseminator of foul misinformation, a vile spreader of objectionable lies that ruin lives—he didn't want to sound like that, having only wanted to heavy-metal in the dark arts just for conversational kicks, which wasn't happening; he said, "I'm not sure if the truth is more important than a good story. I'm not sure that its truth matters anymore, to this day. And how else but this way would I have heard about Gilles de Rais [still pronouncing it Gee day Rah], who in any form could only be a story to me today. I wish he hadn't lost his life over a monstrous lie, of course, sure, absolutely, but the lie that killed him is how I heard about him today, five hundred years later. Death: a rotten path for each of us—fame: for the select."

Real stern, Ronny said, "It was his one life, period. But on top of which, Gilles de Rais [still pronouncing it Zheel duh Ray] was an accomplice to Joan of Arc, not a child killer or demon worshipper—his true self a better story. In addition to all of this, the lie itself is a frickin' tragedy!"

Tommy's frustrations didn't embolden Ronny's resolve, though Tommy felt they did, really what happened was Ronny felt plain sure that Tommy had picked a flawed perspective. Ronny was being a merciful angel of wholesome facts, and Tommy felt trapped and hopeless, continuing to wish the conversation had gone in a different, darker but lighter direction. Tommy nodded, nodded, with the facts in his head now, assuredly, and he did appreciate that facts were being stressed, but he didn't think that facts should feel this distressful. This hadn't been his initial intended conversational trajectory and he said, "Hey—I should've framed the context against Ken Russell's *The Devils*, now I realize."

Ronny hadn't seen *The Devils* but they both wanted the conversation over so they skipped the topic, familiar with this type of interaction between each other.

When the conversation was over it was already over but there was some, hmm, sticky residue. They experienced being stuck in a heavy glob of strained silence, having to think about how to pull themselves out of this, though their mental efforts further stuck them. So Tommy thought to teleport them into another conversation, mentioning how he often called Ronny while walking around the city. And okay at first that seemed curious to bring up, but he was only beginning, as then he thanked Ronny for being a fantastic conversationalist, and thanked Ronny for being alive—so Ronny smiled and things became better from then on, during their remaining time together.

Try this out on your own: when someone becomes frustrated by your general existence, switch into complimenting them, which very often helps, since most people do not want to feel frustrated, but do want to feel complimented. For dessert, since Ronny and Tommy felt like it, they each ordered a yogurt parfait. Then they chatted about their favorite movie according to Tommy, who brought it up each time, *Hackers*, directed by Londoner Iain Softley, starring Angelina Jolie and her first husband.

When they were leaving Scramblers Tommy was still wanting to rekindle their philosophical friendliness that Gilles de Rais had severed, so he introduced a fresh topic by asking a ripe question, "The universe, is it infinite?"

B i n g o—this question interested Ronny and it was immediately evident that this conversation would go over much better; Tommy kept going, "Well, it's hilarious to imagine an infinite number of me. It makes the most sense for me to be the only me, so there must be a finite probability of life in this universe—in fact humans may be a unique specimen in the universe, in terms of time lapsed since the big bang, and the circumstances that enabled our existence.

"It could be we who discover life on other planets(!)."

Ronny nodded because he enjoyed chats about the cosmos. Exploring his own thoughts and feelings Ronny said, "Expansion since the big bang, persistent inflation, will the universe keep inflating? I want to know some physical cosmology, the shape of the universe and if it's flat, open or closed."

They had found their way back to total vibing: how possible. Tommy smiled, shrugged, and said, "It's scientifically accurate to say that humans are cosmic monsters with ontological uncertainty."

Ronny rubbed his hands together. He rubbed his feet against the ground and said, "Now *I* will give *you* something to think about—a thought for later, put it in your pocket," he said. "Humans: not one plural, but a string of singularities."

Tommy felt him on that; that was a good one. Solid. They waved goodbye before they split off toward their respective cars, next seeing each other a couple months later.

While searching for his essential meaning, the reason life was given to him, Tommy lost himself before rediscovering himself the same as he'd been before: every time.

So the search wasn't worth it but he did it regardless, being a curious and optimistic individual not born blessed with an indisputable gift. Tommy was born disreputable and about six other people ever even told him, "I like being your friend." Instead what he often heard was, "You're weird." People would ask him, "Can you clarify?" Then he would clarify and they would say, "We're so different from each other," which would have been Tommy's first guess.

He had to like himself since few others would, though he really would wonder why he was even alive on occasion, but he lived regardless of his search for his essential meaning being embarrassing depending on how you look at it, and all this book cares about is words that resemble Tommy's personality—this chapter being a prime example of *Gem City*'s structure being most influenced by the architecture of the Winchester Mystery House.

The writer is choosing not to disentangle similarities from dissimilarities in this portrait of Tommy and the Winchester Mystery House, since such matters are not of immediate significance, and are bound to distract the reader from the spirit that is the main point. The story behind the famous mansion begins with Sarah Lockwood Pardee meeting and marrying William Wirt Winchester in New Haven, Connecticut, where she was born and bred, where the Winchester family had a business, and where Sarah and William came to live together.

William was the only son of Oliver, an entrepreneur successful in the garments industry: Winchester & Davies Shirt Manufactory. But Oliver's other business was the New Haven Arms Company, which began as a division of <u>Smith & Wesson</u> known for its repeating pistol named Volcanic; having seen its potential, Oliver had purchased the division.

Its potential was first realized by Benjamin Tyler Henry, who designed the Henry repeating rifle in 1860: a lever-action, breech-loading, tubular magazine rifle manufactured for almost six years, with a total production of approximately twelve thousand. Oliver and William shifted their focus to what became named Winchester Repeating Arms Company, and what followed was Model 1866, the first Winchester rifle, Yellow Boy, used in both the Franco-Prussian War and the Russo-Turkish War, and Model 1873, marketed as The Gun That Won The West.

The Winchester family comfortably entered the Gilded Age, before Oliver died in December 1880, and William died in March 1881. Then Sarah inherited a fortune, half owning a hugely successful gun company. Although, having experienced the infant death of her only daughter too, and her eldest sister's recent death, sad phantoms began haunting New Haven, causing her to flee West to begin life anew, as one of the world's richest women: no one able to tell her who to become, it was up to her alone.

Her mansion in San Jose, California, didn't constitute the remainder of her living experience, for example she owned a houseboat dubbed Sarah's Ark also, but her other homes are whole other stories, and this chapter will focus on the Winchester Mystery House, the home in which she perished.

Sarah was a fantastic type of person: philanthropic and eccentric, consumed by unusual ideas and a troubled magnum opus. Women weren't allowed to be architects at the time when she began designing her mansion, and she hadn't formally studied architecture, but she herself decided what mattered to her, and so she became the chief designer of what was first an unfinished two-story wood-frame farm house, but over a span of thirty-eight years transformed into a mansion with one-hundred and sixty rooms (once one-third larger, and with a seven-story tower, before an earthquake in 1906, during which Sarah was trapped in her daisy bedroom by a crumbled chimney).

With a deliberate defiance of precise parameters, and a cluttered style typical of Victorian homes then, it is a Queen Anne mansion, with Eastlake and Stick elements, a touch of Gothic, and a pinch of the Romanesque. Some of its notable traits: intricate parquet floor woodwork, from five types of wood; deeply embedded Lincrusta wall treatment; Tiffany stained glass; wool insulation; three elevators; two basements; forty-seven fireplaces and seventeen chimneys; thirteen bathrooms; staircases with thirteen steps; rooms with thirteen windows; chandeliers that hold thirteen candles; spiderweb windows; doors that open to a dead end; a second-floor door that leads to a fall outside; skylight windows embedded in a floor; a staircase that leads to a closed ceiling; a Grand Ballroom with gold and silver chandeliers, an organ, a fireplace, and beside its fireplace two art-glass windows inscribed with quotes from Shakespeare:

one, "Wide unclasp the tables of their thoughts," from *Troilus and Cressida* (IV:5:60); two, "These same thoughts people this little world," from *Richard II* (V:5:9). To a casual observer the meaning of the quotes can seem unclear, but they had personal meaning for Sarah—as everything here did.

An intelligent lady raised proper, Sarah learned four languages as a child, and about music, math, and Shakespeare; curiosities about her relate to, for example, what she knew of Rosicrucianism, how much a fan of ciphers she was, and whether she adopted Francis Bacon's numerological methodology. The Winchester Mystery House's facts and fantasies become entangled by descriptions of it, and one example is a room at the mansion's center, called the séance room by those attracted to the idea of Sarah as a spiritualist, or the sanctum, a chamber of reflection, by those attracted to the idea of Sarah as a cultist. She carried the only key to this central room with its one entrance and three exits, and this is said to be where she communicated with spirits at night, receiving the next day's design plans, which she gave her foreman in the morning.

While designing her labyrinth mansion, Sarah is said to have dismantled, built around, and sealed over rooms that failed her expectations. She would tear down and rebuild or abandon elements while chasing what captivated her creative attention, designing an architectural freak show with non-professional and non-precise standards. Even while being built there were outsider observations about why it was how it was, and what type of person Sarah was. Local papers of her time presented her as a ghost-obsessed spiritualist feeling haunted by the spirits of those killed by a Winchester rifle. It was said she designed the house to confuse the spirits chasing her, and kept building in order to keep living, along with more absurdity that seemed verifiable from the mansion's strange architecture. Sarah was an eccentric recluse who often ignored social, religious, and business expectations, and the peculiar facts of her mansion have inspired its legend, and participated in the conjuring of Sarah as a person.

More complexities involved in fully understanding the mansion: perhaps aestheticism inspired the motif of spiderweb windows, but also spiderweb windows are in the thirteenth bathroom, and that might be numerological but it cannot be accidental, since Sarah signed her will thirteen times. And when outsiders observe the mansion's switchback staircase, with its two-inch-high rise, they do not immediately think of this staircase being built for her convenience, owing to her rheumatoid arthritis and fifty-eight inch height. Other misperceptions about the mansion relate to disrepairs not amended following the 1906 earthquake. Certainly the earthquake disrupted the mansion, toppled its seven-story tower, collapsed its fifth and sixth floors, and discontinued expansion of the north wing. Unlike many on her neighbors, Sarah chose not to rebuild or repair her mansion. The doorway to nowhere was meant to lead to another section. A stairway to a ceiling was meant to lead to another floor. It was left looking as if created by a madwoman, which Sarah realized and had mentioned.

Though the skylight windows embedded in the floor are difficult to explain from any perspective. But Sarah didn't have to explain anything to anyone; the mansion was a manifestation of her personality, a higher dimensional puzzle expressing her own tastes and interests, a living art piece made during the Gilded Age—that was all.

The mansion developed a reputation for being haunted while being constructed, and now it is perceived as definitely haunted. Following Sarah's death in 1922, what came of the mansion was that John Brown and his wife Mayme leased it for ten years as a business enterprise. Previously, John had invented one of the earliest roller-coaster cars, the backety-back; he switched from building amusement park devices to owning the mansion because of the mansion's name and reputation.

Mayme was the original tour guide, when the mansion opened to the public, five months after Sarah's death. Harry Houdini, having heard about this place, in order to debunk its myth he visited it in 1924; although he didn't debunk the myth that began to swell.

It wasn't completed all at once, the myth of this mansion. The number thirteen became a popular conversational topic in 1929. How many of the rumors about the number thirteen are true? One may notice that the chandeliers capable of holding thirteen candles are poorly designed, not reflecting Sarah's own fine tastes.

The Browns ended up purchasing the mansion, and still to this day they own it, under the company name Winchester Mystery House, LLC. In the 1970s Keith Kittle became the mansion's manager; he came from Frontier Village, a family-run western-style amusement park. He installed the Winchester rifle museum in the mansion. Along the freeway he put up red, white, and black billboards that had a skull, which became successful marketing that helped shape the mansion's myth. Kittle brought the mansion into the National Register of Historic Places, and into the Library of Congress, as part of the Historic American Buildings Survey, under this description—

> Significance: This extraordinary structure is *sui generis*. Constructed over a period of 38 years because its owner, Winchester Rifle heiress Sarah L. Winchester believed she would live as long as construction continued, the house contains 160 rooms and covers six acres. The original portion purchased in 1884 contains 17 rooms. Some of the 40 stairways and 2,000 doors lead nowhere.

The mansion has received millions of visitors since Sarah's death, and now it has a year-long membership program called the Skeleton Key Club. And there's a mansion tour offered every Friday the 13th, along with the Halloween Candlelight tour.

It's not a perfect mansion, and Sarah wasn't exceptional in constructing a house of great complexity, but lots of people want perfection and only Sarah wanted what Sarah wanted.

****

Crucial reference material: *Captive of the Labyrinth: Sarah L. Winchester, Heiress to the Rifle Fortune* by Mary Jo Ignoffo

When Tommy was off from work he noticed that Alexander had texted an emoji of a satellite, so Tommy replied with an emoji of a wizard.

This was six p.m. and the sun had set at five fifteen —one might guess Tommy to be fond of early sunsets, being such a tremendous fan of nights and all, but that would be incorrect. His heart preferred the bonus nighttime following nine-o-clock summer sunsets, when he could stay up past one or two with ease—that number of hours following winter sundowns converted into staying up until nine or ten, which caused him to become too tired too early, and made him feel like he was missing out—which could be a symptom of winter blues or seasonal affective disorder, Tommy called it unavoidable.

That night like usual he experienced life by reading: having recently finished Mikhail Bulgakov's *The Master and Margarita*, a narrative that explores dimensional concepts in a vivid literary dreamscape, a robust classic that Tommy treasured:

> 'And where are you, ma'am?'
>
> 'I'm nowhere,' answered Margarita, 'I'm your dream.'
>
> 'I thought so,' said the boy.

Tommy had then begun reading Terrance Raven's *Exit 666,* which wasn't of the same writing caliber, but Tommy knew that before going in. Would he accept it for what it was? What was there to accept: a book written by a contemporary young imaginative person calling themself Terrance Raven. A genderqueer Wisconsin writer beginning their career by writing a book of bizarro fiction. Tommy was into the signs of his time, like bizarro fiction, and he was reading *Exit 666* because often after a big book he enjoyed a breezy read, a short book, a novella. Novellas are short enough that each is a chance worth taking. Except, not all! But Tommy took risks reading contemporary writers who hadn't been stamped by excellence over time since he searched for the same things as other readers: further writerly imitations of complex human behaviors developing across time and culture. It is common for a reader to desire a writer who shares a temporal reality with them, the writer growing the reader's perspective of a shared reality.

How was *Exit 666*? Eh. Tommy had read worse and better. He was at the part when the wizard motorcyclist flees the cannibal elves: chapter one, page eight. It was then that he received a text from his friend Carmilla, whom he hadn't heard from in several months.

She texted that in about an hour she'd be leaving from her company's holiday party, and did he want to watch a movie with her? Although sometimes being utterly alone actually felt like a better idea to Tommy, he did want to watch a movie with Carmilla. He asked if she wanted to watch *La Strada*, which he had recently thought sounded like a movie they'd watch together.

She texted that she'd never seen *La Strada*. He texted that it's a classic so worst case she'll have seen it. Carmilla expressed laughter via text, texting yes to *La Strada*. He asked when. She told him, it wasn't too long from then.

So he finished reading a paragraph from *Exit 666* before he started getting ready early, giving himself plenty of time to get ready, because he never liked getting ready, and this way he could meanwhile sneak in more reading. Hankering for a glimpse at where *Exit 666* was headed, wondering if he should finish it, Tommy didn't read the end of *Exit 666* but he did glance at it while brushing his teeth. The end didn't feature the wizard motorcyclist, holy rabbit, the final chapter appeared to take place at a coven, but also a centaur paced the room.

Wait, why, what—the very end took place inside a witch's head that was populated by other witches(!), and oh my, the cerebral witches caught the head on fire:

> Amid the flames the fire starters did not burn
> but giggle and dance.

Very not what Tommy had anticipated. Was it a metaphor for the imagination? How one's imagination brings flames to their brain? His eyes scanned a line on the next paragraph:

She was melting and her eyes boiled.

The ending was literal, this genre wasn't into metaphors, a coven of witches had started a fire inside another witch's head, which melted her: simple fact.

Tommy was into writers who recognize the imagination as lawless and possibilities as infinite. But he wasn't absolutely positive the prose style of *Exit 666* would grip him. He considered the writing unaware of how to shine.

In addition, this particular shape-shifting narrative wasn't moving enough to pique Tommy's curiosity.

A central problem with both the prose and narrative was clumsy execution.

After Tommy put on an acceptable social shirt, then he returned to his bookmarked page of *Exit 666*, desiring not to give up on this book he began reading two days prior by the way. Two days later he'd be on chapter three, and four days later he'd begin reading another book. It brought him no joy to give up on a book—especially novellas, the short ones!—but his reality didn't often cater to his wishes, and not every book was for him. He most desired to read everything, anything, at least a little from all of it, only not worrying about reading *everything* since he knew he never could, he read and read with no plans to stop, and yet Tommy finishing a book felt exactly like Tommy making a friend: he wasn't against any person, though some people became his friends and some didn't, just as he wasn't against any book, though he finished reading some and not others. He never stopped loving books but didn't always know, couldn't always guess, which book he'd read next, or which book he'd finish. He wanted to find the good inside each person, and each book, but sometimes other details consumed his thoughts; his reading and friendship depending to equal degrees on his mood and the mood of the book/person by the way.

Tommy searched for harmony between himself and other people, and books, with nothing guaranteed but expansive possibilities. While reading about the elven cannibals catching and devouring the wizard motorcyclist, which concluded chapter one, Carmilla texted that she was home.

Heading across McLain to Keowee, going toward 5th, Tommy cruised familiar sidewalks important to him, while exploring the frontiers of his thoughts and feelings like always. Except it was 8 p.m. and he was almost tired: uh-oh—see. It was cold but he felt fine wearing winter clothes, and from headphones he heard Brian Eno sing "Golden Hours."

So Tommy walked and time walked, his restless mind feeling soothed by the wind, his life moved toward and away from him.

No one cared.

But Carmilla was expecting him.

Though because of his drifting thoughts, and owing to unspoken urges, Tommy found himself inside of Bonnett's Book Store by accident. He wanted to see if they had a used copy of *The Halfway House* by Guillermo Rosales, which novel he read about recently. Though they didn't have it, which was too bad Tommy thought. He mentioned his disappointment to an employee who said it definitely wasn't in the back but could be special ordered. Outside after the special order Tommy thought about having to wait to open the book he wanted to open right then: ughck. Walking in frustration he headed in the wrong direction; the city smelled like werewolf underwear and a train passed over the 5th Street bridge.

So he walked a couple blocks in the wrong direction owing to misguided thoughts, but after realizing he was walking the wrong way he turned around. Just a lousy moment of misspent energy and wasted time. But nothing so heavy it could crush him. In fact it had been so insignificant he viewed it as funny rather than terrible.

It was cold but not too cold, it'd been colder and he'd felt colder. While headed in the proper direction, Tommy briefly thought he might as well become abducted tonight. Why not? What was stopping them? It was a spontaneous thought about what was possible on this cloudy night, since his grandmother couldn't see him from the moon, so she couldn't protect him and aliens could abduct him. He began praying: "Dear God, if you're real, and aliens are real, abduct me. If only you're real, create aliens and have them abduct me: this is all I'll ever ask of you."

Knock knock. Carmilla opened her door and there she was. Then Tommy was on her couch and now she asked him a question related to marshmallows.

Next he held a mug of hot chocolate, with only a few marshmallows, which was how he liked it.

Carmilla, still in the kitchen, asked if Tommy liked her furniture. He said he did. She mentioned it was more than vintage: her furniture had personal meaning. This Furniture Had Been My Grandmother's, she said. He said he liked her furniture, and vintage furniture in general. She said her previous boyfriend said he didn't. He noticed she mentioned her ex-boyfriend and he thought about that out loud. She said Oh He Just Said That.

Tommy wiggled on the couch and turned his eyes toward a wooden record player. Then Carmilla was next to him with her own hot chocolate, and they began talking about things they could talk about, such as books and movies.

Besides books and movies what they had in common was having seen each other a few other times. This was an evening between friends and not filled with romantic hope for either of them. They met a spell of years ago, through a circumstantial origin story being omitted to save time and space. What's being mentioned is they'd never made promises to each other, and the context of their friendship was they saw each other on an irregular basis.

They chatted about the books and movies they could, before sharing a few nice and light stories from their past together, not too many stories, because they didn't have many, but remembering the ones they did.

Followed by a gap of silence.

Hmm.

Knowing *La Strada* to be full screen, Tommy thought to ask, "Do you adjust your tv settings for full screen movies?"

Carmilla said, "What?"

He laughed not at her but at his question. He said, "I didn't know anything about this until a friend told me, and he told me well after I should have known. Some movies are full screen and some are widescreen, and these widescreen tvs can be adjusted for full screen movies. It makes a difference."

She said, "Do we have to change it?"

"No," he said, and they didn't. And he didn't care because the point was he felt lucky having a friend who'd watch *La Strada* with him.

Carmilla and Tommy's movie watching tradition was to discuss the scenes while team-building ideas about characters and story. *La Strada* is about a traveling entertainer whose companion died before the beginning, and from the mother of his dead companion he purchases another. The entertainer, Zampanò, is a strong man. His new companion is Gelsomina, who learns to play a drum in order to announce the beginning of his performances. Tommy was into carnival culture. Carmilla didn't have that specific interest but appreciated culture in general. She noticed a striped shirt and brought up the history of striped shirts. She mentioned that stripes used to be for prisoners, clowns, prostitutes, and hangmen. Then, using her phone, she looked up striped shirts on Wikipedia, to fact check herself, like Tommy would. Carmilla discovered that she had been one-hundred percent correct. She elaborated with details about Queen Victoria bringing stripes to sailors, and Coco Chanel bringing stripes to fashion; stripes being a symbol of rebellion against an ordered world.

Tommy and Carmilla considered Gelsomina mad cool. They guessed her meant to be fourteen. Giulietta Masina, the wife of director and co-writer Federico Fellini, plays her.

Zampanò is Anthony Quinn, who was born in Chihuahua, Mexico, as Antonio Rudolfo Oaxaca Quinn; Tommy's favorite Anthony Quinn movie was *Requiem for a Heavyweight*—which was written by Rod Serling, whom Tommy appreciated through nearby-Antioch College affiliation, and the creation of *The Twilight Zone,* though Tommy didn't mention such outside details right then.

One thing that happened was Carmilla and Tommy shared a brief discussion in regard to the dialogue in *La Strada* being dubbed, and all Italian films at that time being dubbed.

Gelsomina and Zampanò cross paths with a traveling circus, encountering an entertainer of humorous proclamations: a fool. The Fool and The Strong Man are together. They become immediate enemies. The Fool picks on Zampanò, which bad idea causes Zampanò to react with his own bad ideas. Tommy and Carmilla discussed who was worse: The Fool or Zampanò. Carmilla couldn't stand The Fool and Tommy couldn't either. Just something about him. Zampanò had clear problems: he definitely beat Gelsomina after she fled from him but still The Fool was bothersome. Definitely they were each terrible in a different way.

While the movie played Carmilla kept moving around on the couch, shifting positions, until at one point she lay next to Tommy, who wondered why, and so he asked, "Do you want me to lie next to you?"

She turned to him, paused, gave some unreadable face that was worth a thousand sad words, and shook her head no. He felt embarrassed but the moment passed. Anyway all night he felt embarrassed about his canker sore.

Being with Carmilla was for Tommy like being around a longtime friend, except in a different way, because of less time together, but equal degrees of mutual understanding despite dissimilar particulars.

Carmilla was an accomplished professional whose job allowed her to live alone in a single bedroom luxury apartment. Her job was one that Tommy knew some other women and men would want to have: the district manager for a chain of movie theaters. She was single, somehow, but not the one for him, for some reason; and she felt the same about him. They'd never said anything else. By the end of *La Strada* they agreed it was solid but not one of their favorite movies ever. Zampanò ended up becoming the clear worst.

Tommy left not long after the movie ended, walking back home in the cold dark night and wondering if Zampanò had been any shred of good at all. He offered Gelsomina a life path to early death. Why had Tommy liked Zampanò in any way?

A quality Tommy appreciated was when a great movie was brought to further life in his thoughts and feelings.

It began snowing, which Tommy didn't feel one way or another about, only noticing what's being mentioned.

Tommy worked a mid-shift, later strolling the snowy brick roads of 5th St. until back in his room, when and where his mother called him.

Tommy learned that his niece who reminded him of himself had been arrested, same age as when he had been. Her crime was related to a goat, he'd learn more about this later.

And his mother mentioned having started writing a new book, with herself as the main character again, but this one would be fiction. What it would be was she would be watching a movie alone in a theater, and she'd realize the movie was about her—and not wanting to watch a movie about her she'd leave this theater for another: there would be six other screens with six other movies about the lives of six other women, for example Helen Keller and Anne Sullivan ("I was actually more impressed by Anne Sullivan"), Maya Angelou, Sobonfu Somé, and this would be written as fan fiction. Tommy's mother would write herself as a ghost who meets other women who become part of a shared journey, and for example there would be a moment when Hedy Lamarr tells Anne Frank that if the Navy had listened to her about spread spectrum communication then everything would have turned out differently for her and many others during WWII—and all the women would have a conversation together at the book's end, discussing how to look at life from a positive perspective. The point would be to see the good amid the bad, and learn from the movies of others—his mother said that people so often only care about their own movie.

Her inspiration for this book came from the book fair she went to for *Hellhole*. A year before she had brought *One Little Black Book* to this book fair too, and it had won the top prize. But this time with *Hellhole* the writer who won a) wrote fiction not non-fiction, and b) wrote about a thirteen year-old girl having a conversation with Annie Oakley. "You believe that?" Tommy's mother said. She said she heard about that Annie Oakley book and thought, "Wow," believing herself possessing far more expansive writing capabilities. Listening to a cd of Don Miguel Ruiz's *The Four Agreements* had inspired the concept of hopping between theaters; the ghost format introduced to her at the book fair's writing workshop.

She was five pages from finishing the book before the coffee truck opened five days from then. "It gets hot here, so I shaved my hair," his mother told him.

"I want to tell you three stories about other people reacting to my shaved head," she didn't say before she told him such.

By this time it was known that *Hellhole* hadn't cracked into the top one hundred sales chart, despite international efforts. And *My Autobiography Is My Manifesto: Volume One* had been published but only purchased by some family and friends mentioned in it, not even purchased by some people mentioned, and zero feedback regardless. Marketing? One in a plethora of things Tommy had heard about without knowing about. Already behind him, the publishing of *My Autobiography Is My Manifesto: Volume One* felt like a minor catastrophe. Tommy did realize some of what went wrong, and yet still he thought there was more to it than what was wrong (more than the obvious); but he didn't market it and few people read it, nobody cared about it anyway.

Then: all he himself could think to do was continue writing as well, definitely in the blood and everything. He had begun thinking about writing a new book about himself, one that would be fiction but still about him, the type of writing he had just heard his mother describe in fact, this idea had been in his mind too, which he found interesting, and perhaps symbolic of order amid the chaos, although also maybe just a phantom pattern.

Tommy's life felt both outrageous and as if happening for a specific reason

Brett turned thirty-three on a mid-March Tuesday.

Isabel, the woman he loved, organized his birthday party for that Saturday.

Excited by this, Tommy and Roscoe drove three-plus hours to Brett and Isabel's one-bedroom second-floor apartment in Cleveland, Ohio.

While motoring their way they reminisced upon meeting Brett at the beginning of a new school year years ago, on a Kent State University dorm stoop, immediately bonding with Brett through traditional, magical human magnetism, 'trouble finds trouble,' back when Brett shared beers from his black backpack.

Tonight Brett and Roscoe and Tommy would be the same people they had been back then: the times changed but the magnetism remained the same—they aged and their fights changed but their fighting remained the same.

Tommy and Roscoe ignited their interior selves while thinking about this out loud together. They sure felt revved up.

Although unfortunately, typically, upon party arrival Tommy realized his excitement had been theoretical and related to general concepts like old friendships and Brett being alive actually.

From a lens of reality the party became a personal problem for Tommy who met the other attendees and they all seemed totally normal; he felt wrecked, just kidding but for real.

By Tommy's nature, he didn't want to do the things one does to make normal people happy. Normies considered Tommy tricky but it was mutual, since the too-easy was tricky for Tommy to tolerate.

Normies talk about normal things but not fucking Tommy who favored the holy lights of extravagant and introspective melodramas stemming from the emotional complexities of the human condition, which Roscoe, Brett, and Isabel understood, felt similar about, that was three people, a party challenge was nine others: Brett's friends whom Tommy didn't know.

But special occasion, Brett's birthday party, so Tommy worked against letting himself appear anguished.

He dealt with this situation how he dealt with things: he sat alone on a torn dirty beige leather recliner in the living room's back left corner, able to view the whole room free of pressure, feeling unconcerned about circumstances unrelated to him, and appreciating this night's intention without feeling the responsibility to do a damn thing: chilling.

He hadn't made an oppressive commitment to the poker table across the living room and next to the kitchen: Brett and Roscoe with four others, on red plastic chairs around a red plastic table. They engaged in chitchat, nothing too fussy, too much to handle, or anything Tommy found compelling. Did they talk about anything related to their essential meaning? Nah.

Throughout the whole night Tommy never heard any intimate speculations regarding existence within a spiritual world.

To his immediate left, below a remarkable painting that'll be further elaborated upon later, four people on a beige leather couch chatted about things that fit inside their life context and made sense to them at the time: delicious but petty dramas involving people they knew—heavy observations they released to lighten themselves. Tommy attempted to appear friendly by nodding to each speaker whatever they said.

And there was another beige leather recliner at the sofa's other end, identical to Tommy's except not torn, and with a memory foam pad, to be honest it was superior. A person on the identical-but-superior beige leather recliner chatted with a crossed-legged person who sat with their back against a cluttered trunk table. These two were speaking of sports; Tommy made no comment.

Tommy began feeling lost amid the typical at a basic birthday party.

But the situation didn't call for him to panic, so he didn't.

What he did was act better than natural, super calm, extra casual, having appeared untroubled for an hour or so; nice.

Pure will power and concentration.

Emotional sorcery.

Hovering above the abyss.

Secretly longing for a party that took place in essential meaning, he'd never been to a party like that; he'd been to parties like this—back when he was a teenager, he'd already partied like this.

Everyone smoked cigarettes and drank beer.

The apartment smelled like smoke and dirty feet.

Tommy took a drag from a cigarette Isabel had given him.

Two tubes of fluorescent light stretched from above the poker table into the living room's middle, and a lamp shaped like a white whale shone from a corner table between the sofa and Tommy's recliner. And owing to this luminescence Tommy noticed colossal stains on the living room's cream carpet: he considered picking up two red plastic cups fallen on the floor but they were fine he figured, and he didn't want to pick them up regardless, since he wasn't in the mood and the situation didn't call for it; the living room reminded him that the most righteous path to a mellow state comes through acceptance.

Mellow is the best part of life, Tommy was certain.

He only wanted to worry about what he had to.

In fact this living room's junky benevolence originated from Brett and Isabel's own lack of fear about what was or wasn't worth worrying about. They were prone to forgive flaws that'd be better if non-existent, and far more likely to accept a flaw than complain about it; Brett considered this rational because he found minor irritations distractions from core metaphysical, existential, and whatnot problems that were his primary considerations.

Brett and Isabel related to the full range of potential problems in a massive reality, Tommy and Roscoe related too; they were the usual variety of uncommon people, crazy to everyone not them, filled with outrageous curiosity actually, they made complete sense to each other, and when with each other they could feel proud of how bizarre they were, though things became trickier when around others.

Anyway, being there, sweating nothing momentarily, Tommy eyeballed an enormous purple puddle stain beside his recliner and, feeling tender, he said, "My dear friend Brett: who created this marvelous purple stain?"

Brett replied, "Yeah, what?"

Isabel leaned over from the end of the couch and patted Tommy on his knee; she shrugged. She said, "No one knows what happened, sometimes we don't remember the nights."

Tommy shrugged.

Brett said, "Hey, hey hey hey, hey real quick, hey, hey," he turned toward Tommy, "You'll like this.

"You're asking me because you want to hear it, since you already know it, and I can't wait to tell you.

"So after the first few carpet stains appeared I lost my cool and became hella upset, you can imagine.

"But then another stain appeared, and another— and if I lose all my cool I'm fucked in life.

"So I had to find a way to maintain my cool.

"I concentrated.

"I lifted my thoughts above my feelings— sometimes you have to be counterintuitive in that way, and fight against your first feeling.

"That's one way to do it and I did it, building myself to a point where I could stop worrying about the stains.

"Since in terms of how awful life can become, carpet stains are small potatoes.

"My life perspective is lighter now that I am free of such a ridiculous worry as carpet stains. There are real burdens in this world, and those are the ones I wish to overcome."

Brett turned back to the poker table, slammed down his cards, exposed himself as the winner, raked in the jackpot, there was a gasp, that was fantastic.

Tommy smiled at the purple puddle stain, staring into it but noticing nothing significant, that was a wacky thing to do, he was acting his kind of normal.

Conversations continued among everyone not Tommy, whose eyes had been drawn in by the eyes of a snow leopard perched atop a mountain cliff below a full blood moon: the painting above the couch.

The painting looked glowy, likely made with contemporary paint materials that shined in black light. It held radiance. Cheap radiance. Still radiance.

The snow leopard peered from the painting into Tommy's eyes, and the stare felt truly transcendent.

Tommy began feeling mystical.

He thought-whispered: Majestic Snow Leopard, You're Inspirational.

His lifted spirits put him in the mood to participate in a party conversation he listened to:

"George is awful, but Tracy is worse than awful. Never trust someone named Tracy, just as never fear someone named Larry."

"Mmm—you're making me feel religious and here's why: Tracy considers his every contemptuous thought an absolute fact, and it's horrible because he says brutal things without making a joke or being intentionally mean: hallelujah about Fuck That Guy. How can he think he sees so much when he has no compassion, no sympathy, no emotion—he doesn't understand the best parts about being human!"

"Yesssss, and he's twins with Clarence, but Clarence is the eviler of the evil twins. I mean it. Oriah won't divorce him because she truly loves him, but she knows it too. Between just us she's pregnant and Clarence is a cold-blooded individual with an atrocious life perspective, their kid's future life perspective is royally doomed. Let me tell you: Clarence is full of pride for himself and contempt for others. You should hear him talk about how much he hates the world and the people in it. Hate, like love, is a personal condition. He hates many, many people for making this world much, much worse, convinced he knows why the world should be hated, everyone not him pissing him off—so very certain about being pissed off that other pissed-off people look up to him, consider him strong! They're pissed off too, and he becomes their leader! People who find aggression inspirational bring me into states of depression. No one pissed off should be making any kind of decision, ever, because never choose force over tenderness and intelligence, I'm saying. Clarence judges everything he sees and he's prepared to be upset his entire life—I'm not making this up."

"I do think Oriah looks up to aggression. She sees anger as power, like you said. I want to kidnap their baby and teach love, don't tell Oriah because she wouldn't approve, she doesn't like me. We don't get along."

Over ensuing silence, Tommy felt a problem with the fact that there had been a conversation about who was the worst of three terrible people. He thought this illustrated people as more complicated than a concept. People: not concepts but complexities, begging for simplicity but not simple. And from this underlying perspective, related to some people having to say what others would not say, okay, Tommy would be on the conversational side of the despised, since he felt that someone had to be, so it would be him when it was no one else: this was a central component of his personality, let it be extrapolated: Tommy manifested being on the side of the despised in all sorts of social situations, influencing the complex reality he shared with others—there he was experiencing these unspoken urges and, intending to shift the focus of the conversation away from putting people down for whatever reason, hoping to turn the conversation in a positive direction (which it sounded as if this crowd of people would be totally into), Tommy asked, "Compared to Clarence, is George a good person?"

Wow, immediately he detected they considered his question misguided, conveyed by both their silence and physiognomy.

The person on the middle of the couch thought to say, "They're all headed to hell."

A person at the poker table said, "The scale was from bad to worst."

The person on the superior-recliner summarized, "To directly answer your question: George can be seen as less bad, but not more good."

What a perceptive room.

Tommy smiled and nodded while becoming a better listener. Being a bad listener wasn't good sense. He left himself two mental Post-it notes:

Read the tone of the room.

Become the snow leopard.

Oh, he had left that note before, he realized. The one about the snow leopard, from the last time he visited this apartment. So he also made a note about reading the Post-it notes on the fridge, leaving it above the light switch as he departed from his mental kitchen.

The party conversation had enlarged its shittalking into a broader context, a full demographic being described as Satan's children.

Certainly Tommy felt as if overhearing party conversation topics dissimilar to his favored perspectives.

Crystal clear: his personality wasn't party-material, and he most related to other people who also felt too baffled by society to become a part of it.

Okay: all that combined, in that instance, not knowing how the night might change, Tommy remembered he could change himself, and what happened was the party was transpiring when a person from the couch decided to leave, and it was like a ray of sun between a crack in the clouds, for this was a near-perfect opportunity for Tommy to sneak in a brief stroll.

"Let me walk you out," Tommy said to the person leaving.

"I'm fine," the person said.

"Let me walk you to greatness," Tommy said.

The person laughed so Tommy's plan became possible, that was a close miss.

"You're beautiful," Tommy said to the person on their way out the door.

Tommy walked the person to their car and said goodbye, that was taken care of and went as well as it could have.

Then the wind whispered to him as he fulfilled his personal desire to stroll alone.

On a waxing gibbous moon he could see Mare Crisium, his grandmother's front lawn, so he waved to her.

Truth be told, he would've preferred an extra-long stroll that fostered a grand interior spectacle which culminated in an operatic revelation of perspective-shifting proportions, but for only about seven minutes he strolled alone outside the apartment complex, mostly thinking about nothing.

After not too long he was back inside the party, sitting again on the torn dirty beige leather recliner, feeling lighter after being alone, zero people asking him any possible question, which was terrific except he suffered brief paranoia related to feeling like nobody cared about him.

He sat there ready to answer any question anybody might ask him, there being many possible questions somebody might ask him, but nobody asked him anything, which worried him until he remembered what he often forgot, that people weren't against him so much as not thinking about him—he wasn't the point of this night.

His paranoia slowly subsided.

The birthday party wasn't challenging, he was.

This birthday party wouldn't become a problem unless he made it one, so he didn't.

The party people continued being the type of people familiar with the art of being social among friends at a party, which Tommy read about and saw in movies.

In real life he sat there and pondered what he felt it best to ponder that night, which was nothing.

Choosing to chat with nobody, his non-chattiness wasn't interrupted thank God. He avoided eye contact for personal safety, feeling mega mellow and relaxed in a state of nothingness, fully pretending to be nothing but a chill guy at a party, really pulling it off somehow.

Then *knock knock* and no one knew who it was: the cops?

It turned out to be the opposite of a catastrophe: two of Brett's friends dressed as creatures, one tiger and one moth, which, based on common sense, everyone conversationally appreciated upon entry.

Followed by additional traditional preliminary conversational material: I've Missed You; I Love You; Yeah It's Getting Colder Outside; Do You Want A Drink.

One aspect of the human condition is accepting life never being too surprising really.

Tommy didn't mention this but had the thought: a wonderful party surprise would've been if these creatures had brought a costume for everybody.

The normies performed normal talking routines that Tommy never enjoyed because it was bullshit okay, and he would rather starve to death than eat those fruits, just kidding but for real.

At this point he thought: Birthday Party Rattle My Soul, I Dare You, before remembering to avoid thoughts about feeling bothered: that's right.

He switched his thoughts back into feeling nothing again, which was way better again.

But then as if from nowhere, yet really within the night's limited possibilities, the tiger brought a conversation to Tommy.

With a smile under tiger makeup, whiskers on his cheeks, and in a deep warm voice the tiger asked Tommy what he thought about a recent news item of particular interest: the detainment of shark finning poachers off the Galapagos coast.

Yes of course: Tommy had heard this news, as everybody who regularly reads *National Geographic* had. It was terribly sad news but Tommy felt the conversational point was not to be kind so much as appear kind, and he wasn't about to play the game of making being kind seem as easy as noticing the obvious.

So, responding to what he considered meretricious compassion, Tommy said, "Bummer" to play along a little, but real flat and with a deadening force that expressed conversational disinterest.

Sure enough: not the tiger's desired response.

The tiger said, "I feel extreme sympathy. Poachers dump these finless sharks into the ocean, where they're eaten from defenselessness or sink to their deaths. Terrible!"

The tiger was aware of what he had said and what it meant, so he waited only a moment before a poker player soon said, "People are monsters."

The tiger nodded with firm conviction, feeling as if not having asked for too much, and having received his desired response. "Thank you."

Tommy silently wondered about the poachers: why did they poach, from necessity or pleasure, and was desperation ever an excuse for the terrible—poaching was intolerable, were poachers too; Tommy locked eyes with the snow leopard.

This was shouted by a person at the poker table: "One only ever hears horrible news," followed by widespread agreement.

Tommy felt that was way true and considered this party conversation a particle of the problem.

Another story related to animal cruelty was mentioned (a roommate cooking another roommate's pet ferret), and the party conversation continued along but Tommy wasn't interested in further listening, seeking to avoid contributing his perspective that might arouse suspicions regarding his attitude— he didn't want to seem against this party he wasn't into.

In order to forge an internal path toward better appreciating other people, Tommy began remembering cognitive biases on his mind from having read about them several days prior. He blankly stared at nothing, nodding when others did, specifically recalling: the bias blind spot (recognizing the biases in others while failing to see one's own); the trait ascription bias (viewing one's own personality as variable and the personalities of others as predictable); the extrinsic incentives bias (viewing the motivations of others as situational and one's own as dispositional); the introspection illusion (considering one right and others wrong); and the attribution bias (systematic errors made when evaluating behaviors by oneself and others).

Immediately upon learning about these things Tommy had been able to tell he should watch out for them in his own behavior.

If anything he wanted the party people to initiate his ingroup bias, but they didn't.

He might've been at a party filled with wonderful people but he couldn't tell.

He knew that some problems he had with the world came from him, but he couldn't always tell which ones, so to soothe himself he began listening to the Lil Peep music playing.

Brett had chosen this music, as both Brett and Tommy often listened to intensely personal music about feeling down.

Most people don't.

Most people think mentioning anything about feeling down is being down.

People who don't like downers probably prefer to talk about shark finning.

Brett and Tommy were fighters who were downers, and downers who were fighters, depending, so, calmly, casually, Tommy began wondering if he could handle being doomed, since he really maybe was doomed for his whole damn life, pondering this while "Crybaby" played.

Lil Peep sang about many people sharing the feeling of wanting to die.

Tommy was into this song that gifted beauty to endless gloom.

He connected with the song, though the tone of the room communicated that the party wasn't vibing it, which made sense to Tommy, since this party didn't make Tommy's kind of sense.

The party people had turned their eyes away from Tommy because they expected nothing from him, the same practical reason he had turned his eyes away from them.

Finding much to disagree with concerning the conversational styles of most ordinary people, how could Tommy's destiny be for anywhere but the outside?

He was outside what mattered to this room.

He was used to this.

He accepted it, some times better than other times, and this time he continued being ultra mellow while Lil Peep began another song, "Beamer Boy."

What transpired: Lil Peep surmounted sadness by scheming and dreaming.

Lil Peep, Gustav Åhr, died when aged twenty-one: Rest In Beats.

And but then what happened after not too long was someone switched to popular dance music and the party monsters cheered.

They were delighted but not Tommy, though he didn't let himself become bothered.

People began dancing: basic party.

Tommy wasn't into dancing, with others or alone —not everything is for everybody.

But he smiled as he dance-walked across the room to check on the poker players.

The winner made a joke about the losers, and the losers laughed because it was just poker.

Tommy smiled and stood there alone but with others, adjusting his perspective, knowing he could change the side of himself that others witnessed, desiring to look toward what felt right that night, which was plenty, such as all these people not killing each other—he was figuring out how to be normal at a normal party, and he recalled a key point within a full perspective: people are how they are because that's the way they are, same as he was how he was because that's the way he was; he patted Brett's back, winked at Roscoe, and spun around, dance-walking to the living room's middle.

Cool: aware that one can express one's soul through dancing, Tommy began dancing.

He was more into other expressions of one's soul, and he didn't dance so much as kind of wiggle and sway, but he was acknowledging what he was missing out on, and participating in dancing to the extent that he could.

Sure: people were glad to see him dance.

It's Really Neat To Dance With A Tiger And Moth.

Yes: people stopped playing poker, started dancing; that was fun.

Minutes later he still didn't like dancing and so he returned to sitting on the torn dirty beige leather recliner, pondering the several ways his personality was similar to the living room's carpet stains.

He triple-checked: nothing special about that purple puddle stain. Could he adore it still he wondered, while adoring it since he wondered that.

He quadruple-checked and realized he related to the purple puddle stain from a meaningful perspective regarding essential meaning.

That fucked-up stain was him.

Worry about it? He was busy loving it.

Not feeling desperate from loneliness, but lonely from desperation, Tommy closed his eyes to explore interior darkness for a short while, which seemed like a good idea at the time, feeling again that he needed this, considering himself a sentient purple puddle stain.

He should've taken another short walk outside alone or gone to the bathroom, or not, it didn't matter, his ephemeral worries weren't worth a penny in an ultimate sense regardless—his interior self only suiting the particular needs of his vanishing nows. By this point Tommy felt dangerously close to not being ultra mellow for no valid reason, and he was listening to voices inside himself for guidance, hoping the voices were helpful—tonight his voices told him to defy expectations by not experiencing a personal emotional crisis related to barely anything, which was helpful.

Agitated by being at the party, he was becoming agitated by everything—how very Tommy. He sat there looking ridiculous with his eyes closed, seeming unfortunate to people not him. Nobody knew what he was thinking while he sat on the torn dirty beige leather recliner calming himself, sitting on his hands, contemplating the structure of his belief system right quick, thinking life outrageous while being outrageous, what a guy—following this, inspired by this, tired by this, Tommy opened his eyes to gaze at the snow leopard again, who was telling him what to do next.

The dancing had paused and people were chatting so, okay, like the snow leopard suggested, Tommy participated in a party conversation related to recent movie releases. It wasn't hard! Thank you snow leopard!

He made positive-sounding comments regarding a movie he hadn't liked much. "I thought it flew by."

Then he heard about a movie he hadn't seen. "I could see it."

Then he remained quiet while hearing about a tv show he hadn't seen, since he couldn't relate to that particular interest, although by principle he treasured hearing anyone made happy by anything.

One person brought up reading a famous author and Tommy didn't read that author but he treasured readers so he smiled and nodded.

Sometimes Tommy could act as if he hated people, or was afraid of them, which he didn't and wasn't, he often remembered after being reminded.

Could this night have been better? Yup.

Could it have been worse? Yup.

Did he have a good time? His life tended to feel fine enough when he let things be what they were, which he sometimes did and often didn't.

A bit later but not too much later, the birthday present   Tommy brought Brett entered a conversation.

It was a blu-ray of the first English-language movie directed by Paolo Sorrentino, *This Must Be The Place,* starring Sean Penn as a preposterous ex-pop star who exists only in the movie and yet feels tuned to a movie reality.

Tommy pegged Penn's character as a classic 'too weird to live, too rare to die' type, which types he related to, something about the character clicking with him, that was why he'd given this movie to Brett, who was into the kinds of thing that not everybody else was into, like Tommy. So when Brett asked if it was a good party movie Tommy said Yeah Sure, without thinking about it too much.

Consequences transpired: *This Must Be The Place* began.

When Harry Dean Stanton describes himself as the inventor of wheels on suitcases, Brett said, "Dude, this isn't a party movie, not even close. But I don't care about that. I like this movie."

Tommy mentioned, "If anyone is unsure about what's going on: Sean Penn left his home in Ireland to become a Nazi hunter in America, after his Holocaust-survivor father died. His father had been searching for one Nazi he never found, and Harry Dean Stanton both invented wheeled suitcases and shared info about the Nazi's location."

Most party people left during the movie, though Brett and Tommy and Roscoe kept watching. Isabel went to the bedroom.

An untamed man at the movie's beginning, by the end Sean Penn takes off his makeup and black clothes and shaves his hair to look like a normal man, which makes his mother smile when she sees him from a window.

So at the end of the movie the weirdo does in fact die.

But he found the Nazi and the Nazi lived.

Huh.

"Let me see if I'm getting this straight: he humiliated the Nazi who humiliated his father, but he did not kill him, since the Nazi said the humiliation of Penn's father was a minor event within the Holocaust? Nazi—sympathy?"

Accurate: they weren't quite sure what to take from the movie with an odd voice.

"A fan of oddity, I think *This Must Be The Place* possesses more oddity than grace, no grace at all really, and grace is another major interest of mine, which affects my reaction to this movie. Despite considering Sorrentino's *The Great Beauty* touched by grace, I don't particularly find sugary portraits of barren American roads graceful. I call such road shots played out, done and moved on from, that's how I feel about the road trip aspect of *This Must Be The Place*."

Brett nodded and everyone else nodded since he had nailed his point.

Roscoe said, "This was my second time seeing it, rented through Redbox first. I feel different about it after this viewing, which is always a good sign, but also I don't feel the need to watch it again, like after the first time."

Everyone shrugged and really no one knew what to think. Tommy said, "Welp, I always enjoy the troubled Hollywood entries of notable foreign directors."

Roscoe said, "Sure."

Brett said, "Thanks," while holding up the blu-ray case and making eye contact with Tommy.

Then Brett woke the party animals up, the creatures who'd fallen asleep in front of the television, the tiger and moth, who turned out to be extraordinarily nice people, both of them, they were woken from the floor and asked to leave, the party was over, no big deal, everything was fine.

Brett, Roscoe, and Tommy walked the creatures outside.

Their breath could be seen in rays of light from street lamps.

After the creatures departed and only they three remained, Brett lit a goodnight joint while beginning a conversation concerning memories from the night's party.

When it was his turn Tommy mentioned sitting around trapped inside his mind for some brief amount of time that felt long; Roscoe and Brett understood.

Brett wondered if he should mention something he wanted to, and what ended up happening was he did mention that Isabel had invited over his old friends, people he saw less now than in his past. "Like you two, except I like you two better. Not all friendships last."

Tommy said, "In terms of how much I can like parties, I considered this one great. And happy birthday."

Brett said, "I like having parties thrown for me. Thanks for driving up."

"Thanks for having us," Roscoe said, that was a nice one.

Then Roscoe stretched while smoking a cigarette. Brett smoked a cigarette and Tommy too. Only Roscoe stretched. They felt released from feeling fucked in life while their night ended, standing together in the street, not afraid or alone; they were quiet, and it was comforting silence.

They already understood each other and didn't need to say anything; they were able to read each other's minds basically.

This was Tommy's favorite part of the party. He became high but still, if asked before the party to guess what his favorite part would be, this would have been his guess.

All Tommy wanted from party people was their quiet moments.

Brett, Roscoe and Tommy were in the past and present at the same time that night; all that had changed with time was horrible reality had smothered many of their hopes. Who was more difficult, them or the world—they believed in each other without the world's approval, and they believed in each other more than they believed in the world. Unable to explain themselves in a practical, worldly sense, they failed a world that failed them, but never through their long friendship had one of them said about the other that this world had no use for them.

They each held the general belief that treasures exist inside each and every person.

Then Roscoe and Tommy said goodnight to Brett, having decided to drive back home this late just for the hell of it. They reached Dayton while the Townes Van Zandt song "Rex's Blues" played over a beautiful sunrise.

And they each slept all day long, never minding when they did, preferring to skip the damn days they could.

The following Tuesday Tommy received a phone call from his sister.

He learned about the criminal accusation against his niece: stealing a goat to practice witchcraft.

Immediately: Tommy wondered if he would ever experience such an extraordinary accusation.

Though the situation was not humorous, for his family had to confront the legal and financial obligations of witchcraft accusations, Tommy later learned, after posting about it on Facebook, and his brother-in-law explaining.

Next his sister asked where their mother was.

Tommy said, "What?"

He learned their mother had fought with her housemate and fled from their condo while saying she was leaving forever.

Tommy immediately called his mother.

She was driving from Oceanside into Laguna Beach, having fled from her housemate after a big fight indeed.

Perhaps his mother had felt uncertain about working at the coffee truck?

Mystery, since Tommy asked for no explanations; he only listened.

Definitely she had finished writing her book, shaved her head, and driven away while not knowing if a better life was ahead of her.

Tommy's mother said all she wanted now was privacy.

Tommy asked her to promise him that she felt fine, and she promised.

Tommy asked her to promise him again, and she promised him again.

Two months later was a month after Tommy's thirty-fifth birthday and spring had ended two days prior, but a joke in Ohio was a snowy day. A joke to Tommy was being a year older for no apparent reason. During these days it felt tricky to live easy because the world felt fucked while Donald Trump was President, there was white supremacy and the climate crisis. By late afternoon Tommy was at Wendy's, which was the calmest way he could think to eat while he felt in disarray.

Wendy's would say to him, "Come to me, Tommy," and he would reply, "Yes Wendy's, I'm on my way now."

An Ohio company, the third largest fast food chain in the USA, following Burger King and McDonald's, did Tommy prefer Wendy's to the bigger two?

Joke of a question.

Serious question: should Tommy have eaten somewhere else though, and not experienced fast food in general, for health benefits?

Partially because Tommy should have been anywhere else was exactly why he was here, per his lifestyle of making decisions based on the not recommended—both fearing and longing for death—

he treasured every aspect of his one life that would end when and how it did.

And he considered Wendy's scrumptious food, far superior to the other fast food chains.

His perception his reality, within Wendy's Tommy sought not thrills but chills, feeling fine-fine-fine. Who else comes here? Anybody. Kids and geriatrics. The poor, the rich, couples, families, people on trips. People who don't want to order but they're with a person who does, maybe ordering a Frosty. People visiting Wendy's through fond memories, for their first time, or as part of their regular life routine—*anybody* could pass through, no restrictions, no major financial impediments, no one ordering judging anybody else, everybody feeling the same as everybody else, this egalitarian atmosphere one of the beauties of the place, in addition to its Frosties and square burgers.

Wendy's was a gateway to the Midwest or rather, if the Gateway Arch in St. Louis hadn't existed then the Midwestern gateway would have been any Wendy's anywhere.

A single man who ate alone, mostly Tommy saw other single men doing the same. The employees knew him well, asking how he was each time they saw him; he asked them the same.

To celebrate the new year he ordered the combo special of four items for four dollars: a Diet Coca-Cola, french fries, four chicken nuggets, and a double-stack burger without pickles. Then Nathanael West's *Miss Lonely Hearts* was open in one hand, and another hand dipped a chicken nugget into honey mustard; nothing felt wrong with the world right then; pleasantness felt effortless.

At a table across from him a father, mother, and one son appeared, frankly, glad to be with each other: genuine, unfiltered family love was taking place inside of Wendy's, unobscured by anything fancy schmancy —a family enjoying being with each other while eating here, that simple.

Tommy only briefly saw them, and yet he placed a photo of them amid the Post-it notes on his mental refrigerator, because when dreaming of being another person not himself he could dream of sitting at that table exactly like that—substituting worries with affection.

Time passed and the entire planet still felt fucked in the same ways it did before and would later, but

Tommy left his worries behind him while eating at Wendy's.

At a register Tommy said goodbye to a customer but he didn't mean it, he was just being courteous, since that was a primary job responsibility.

He was to provide the human kindness that robots and self-checkouts couldn't.

Although it was true that his human self possessed an expansive range between kind and rude.

A part-time employee, Tommy full-time experienced the human condition—familiar with and unafraid of feeling low, able to act casual while feeling down, today everything was fine while he scanned items and considered his depressive attitude being related to but independent from his stubborn nature, neither being helpful, and forgiving himself for personal problems he noticed, longing to grow into a person who mustn't be forgiven.

Was the person Tommy longed to be only a couple years ahead of him? Was that all? Please?

While bagging items he ruminated upon the possibility of never finding the career he needed, despite feeling open to his proper place he'd never heard of.

While putting bags in a shopping cart and wondering what his future might become, tearing off a check and handing it to a customer, he realized yet another time: *What A Pickle Life Is*, having written this on a mental Post-it note once or twice before.

Scanning more conveyor belt items, Luke now bagging, Tommy ruminated upon feeling meaningless in an ultimate sense. He wanted to feel less anxious right then but what tended to happen was either his thoughts came before his feelings or vice versa, point is he couldn't tell himself how to feel, his feelings controlled themselves, and that day his feelings experienced a personal problem stemming from many of his work days feeling similar enough to bother him —he didn't want all these same days that kept happening to him, with even his days off work feeling similar, everything in his life feeling similar to everything else in his life, all his days together feeling like this: similar similar similar simiar simiar similar similar similar similer similar similar simiar similar similar similar similar simila similar similr similar smilar imilar similar simiar similar similar similar similer similar similar simiar similar similar similar similar simila similar similr similar smilar imilar similar similar similar similar similer similar similar simiar similar similar similar similar simila similar similr similar smilar imilar similar similr similar simir similar symilar similar similr similar.

The only exceptions merely typos in the oppressive monotony of identical days—Tommy wanted to escape from his familiarity with an unremitting sameness that melted his faint resolve to endure.

Tommy wanted to allow a person glad to be in this world break free from inside of him.

He was certain that other people would desire being around this other person inside of him covered by who he appeared to be.

As in Tommy was not only the person he was but more, which no one ever believed, with others often not wanting to be around him.

As in the world is tough but Tommy made it tougher and got in his own way, which other people he didn't want to be often mentioned to him—other people with their own problems noticing his.

Tommy had his own set of problems.

He was an emotional person with emotional thoughts, and when he acted as if not wanting to live he was part of his problem with life.

Sometimes Tommy wondered why even bother, recalling the locations of nearby bridges, and considering which was the tallest.

But that day while working at the register and feeling almost-suffocated by general anxiety, featureless boredom, selfish despair, and considering himself headed toward not a better life but lower expectations, he gazed upon the daydream of being happy in a modest life with modest expectations— could he live that way?

He daydreamed that his dream life was taking place in this city not worse than him.

Dayton had some problems but so did he, and like him Dayton worked on the problems it did—after realizing that   his higher expectations came from himself, and aspects of his suffering from his own thoughts, could Tommy appreciate his okay life?

Some many days like this day, once Tommy awoke in the morning, and lasting into his afternoon—this guy—he calibrated the difference between his dreams and his reality.

Since each night brings new dreams, this happened often.

To onlookers, his noticeable calibrations appeared distressing, downright frazzling.

Though after Tommy completed his calibrations he tended to have a fuller and healthier perspective, so each calibration was totally worth it and basically personally necessary.

During Tommy's daily calibrations, during Tommy's Tommy moments, no one could guess what his exact problem was.

All they knew was his usual problem had something to do with finding life uncomfortable if not unbearable from endless and strangely specific perspectives.

Most of his coworkers tended to avoid conversations with Tommy while he was being himself.

Most often most people, coworkers but friends too, family members and everyone who met Tommy didn't desire to feel as he often felt, except when sometimes they did feel that way too, then they would come talk to him, when no one else would talk to them, there was actually no one better to talk to then, and no one better to avoid anytime else.

Feeling normal today, Tommy walked through heavy feelings with ease, meaning his usual strange self was detectable to others.

Working beside new-hire Cynthia, a single mother, a head cashier bound for management, he said to her, "Hey."

She waved and said, "Hey," kept working.

Longtime full-time cashier Clarice was there too: Tommy nodded at her, she nodded back, that was that.

Albert and Luke were baggers.

Tommy said to Albert, "Hey." Still in high school, Albert said "Hey" back, without saying anything else the rest of his shift—most teenagers only tell each other what's going on in their minds and hearts.

A father of two, Luke seemed too old for his bagger position. He was a solid guy so it felt odd that he had this job and not a better one, but Tommy felt that way about himself too, sure. Tommy nodded at Luke and Luke didn't nod back, okay: Luke had once mentioned that nodding made him feel like a prisoner. "Prisoners nod to each other," Luke had said once, but not this day—Luke didn't nod or talk with Tommy this day; he was a good worker and father but not much of a social person.

Each coworker trapped in their own world.

All they had in common with Tommy was a red collared work shirt.

Most of his coworkers were nice people who simply concentrated on working while on the clock, which confused Tommy, who never wanted life to feel like work.

What Tommy could do was at least pretend to have something to say to each of his coworkers whenever he saw him or her, in order to appreciate the fact that the other person was alive and doing their own thing.

So it bothered him when feeling low and/or calibrating, how his coworkers wouldn't pretend to be alive with him.

Tommy wished his coworkers knew less about him, or could handle him better.

But also a goal of his was having a mysterious and shatterproof personality, rather than a pathetic one, wishing to be an aura of magic rather than a stink cloud, so he avoided letting himself become bothered by most people most often not having much to say to him since, well, most of the time he hadn't much to say to them either.

Tommy's life wasn't exceptional, and some days it couldn't be enough for him, though some days it could. He wanted to picture today feeling like enough, desiring to capably handle this conventional and quiet, untroubled Tuesday afternoon that wasn't up to no good like he was.

During his last break, while in the break room, a smiling manager approached him and asked, "Tommy, how are you?"

Tommy wondered why in the hell he hadn't chosen to walk around outside alone, knowing he couldn't begin to explain his emotional state to a manager.

With a casual voice Tommy said, "Thinking about tomorrow, looking forward to the future," which he immediately recognized as weird.

The manager squinted.

So, switching into a positive tone, Tommy rephrased it, "A new day's coming, that's how I'm feeling."

Also odd.

Tommy acted casual because he was used to being himself; having no idea what in the hell was going on the manager smiled.

The manager said, "Aw, okay. But I gotta have you out there smiling and liking your job, Tommy."

The manager elaborated, "Today and every day."

Tommy gave a thumbs up and said, "On it," wishing for their exchange to conclude, aware that he wouldn't perform this conversation the way his manager wanted it to be done—or even how Tommy would make plans to do it—all he could possibly do was blow this.

The manager said, "Yeah well, stay on it," patting Tommy on the back and leaving the break room smiling.

Some also-present coworkers could feel what Tommy was feeling, had felt and experienced this as well, but to them this confirmed their suspicion that they didn't want to get sucked inside his world today. Nobody asked him how he felt, since it was apparent.

Today he was toxic and sat alone while not once smiling, wishing it was a different day and he felt normal-alone.

He finished browsing the internet on his phone, then returned to his register.

A memory of his conversation with the manager lingered in his mind, pushing him further away from feeling better until, feeling maximum bothered by noticing that no part of his day helped him feel better, Tommy remembered that feeling bothered never helped him feel not bothered, and so what he thought to do, all he could think to do, was concentrate on scanning items.

Just did his job.

Not letting bad feelings consume him.

Not wanting to think about how he was feeling.

Choosing not to search for the bad inside himself.

He must not let himself become so consumed by the bad that none of the good remained.

He really wasn't in the mood to have a bad day or make his life worse.

After some minutes, you know what the hell happened?

Tommy completed his calibration.

He was able to look at his reality for what it was, and his reality was the same as it had been, but he was looking at it differently now.

So often he struggled to accept the reality in front of him as the reality in front of him: embarrassing really.

He began smiling at customers but for real; basic compassion is easy.

They smiled back; look at that.

He asked to hear about their days, and when he listened to people they told him so much.

Feeling better than several minutes prior, after his last break and right before he was about to leave work, Tommy's manager witnessed him being a good worker who accepted his job and life for what they were: the manager gave Tommy a thumbs up.

Tommy nodded like a prisoner.

Everything was fine.

Right then at work, knowing he had to do what he had to do, and knowing his life would only be the dream it was, Tommy did his job, which was not so bad or hard really.

Full disclosure: everyday all-day long he preferred feeling positive, but only sometimes did he find it possible; how much easier it was to be with people when one was being easy on people; feeling better helped better things happen; when Tommy changed the world did too.

Driving away from work, Tommy regretted how for a huge portion of the day he'd been acting like it was everybody else's fault that his life could feel awful. He really hated when he often did that. He believed that life is hard, but harder when you act like an asshole. Tommy regretted having acted like such a sourpuss, and aah oops he swelled his day's problems yet again, only letting go of being himself now that he was away from other people—and his letting go of being himself was never fast or easy, since memories of his day's mistakes ricocheted off memories of past mistakes, amalgamating to a personal revelation of being a mistake in his entirety, with every dream of his unobtainable.

This was why he made the mental Post-it notes. He read one:

Worries never help.

Mm, an all-time classic.

What was a guy like Tommy building himself toward becoming?

Insatiable melodrama.

Tommy's feelings about his life and job could become melodramatic, and though he kept realizing worries never help, melodrama kept making them sound highly interesting and full of tremendous potential. The sound of melodrama was the sound of life to Tommy, who considered melodrama emotional realism, since certainly life was not pure fun or all smiles. On top of which, Tommy again-again demonstrated radical favoritism toward anything outrageously human, like melodrama, considering it the dirt of being human, which Tommy would roll around in to his delight.

Thinking about his familiarity with melodramatic attitudes calmed Tommy.

Classical music played from the car radio, was that Schubert, Tommy thought it was.

He untangled his day, revealing himself to himself within his thoughts.

He sensed that everything felt too dreadful to be this dreadful.

What had he been thinking a moment ago, oh—that every dream of his was unobtainable.

And why had that been?

Owing to guilt from acting frustrated during most of his day, including after being specifically asked not to feel frustrated.

Why had he felt frustrated?

Because of an interior melodrama caused by the weight of repetition in his life, a full interior narrative invisible to others.

That night Alexander texted a carousel horse emoji.

Tommy replied with a woman's sandal emoji.

The next day at work Omar said, "Why anything?"

Tommy shrugged and shook his head; they high-fived.

This was a normal day and each co-worker was on their own quest like they better be, best wishes to all of them.

Tommy felt spiritually weak but he couldn't fully determine why.

He felt tired from the previous day but also other things were going on inside of him he could tell.

It's true that some days Tommy could do what many do, which is check to see if a random social moment was a perfect opportunity to seek outsider input regarding irrational personal problems, sharing emotions being a reason to talk with another person, but today Tommy wasn't feeling anything he wanted to tell anybody about anyway, since he couldn't describe it.

Something was building but he didn't know what.

He worked like a robot, unable to calibrate his dreams because his gauge felt broken. He wasn't calibrating he was being quiet, and after work he immediately went to Roscoe's.

Roscoe said, "My back hurts. And maggots were in my kitchen last night." Tommy felt shocked and saddened, but for different reasons than earlier. Though he didn't, couldn't, mention anything about himself to Roscoe right then, still he knew Roscoe understood.

Roscoe said, "I learned to stretch like this," before demonstrating a stretch he learned: Roscoe stretched into a beam of moonlight entering through a crack between window drapes.

He showed Tommy a painting he had been working on: a latex painting of flying angels in hell, one angel's wings on fire, the angels picking up those with raised hands.

"Angels saving those called damned, revolting against the existence of hell," Roscoe said.

Tommy smiled.

Oh: their friends Jeff and Ashley came over too—that was a pleasant surprise.

Ah yes: then Amanda arrived home from work, she had invited Jeff and Ashley over.

Tommy felt comfortable in a room with four other people, which was an uncommon circumstance in his life.

He winked at Sukie, who had just winked at him first.

Though after returning to his bedroom later, still Tommy felt a certain internal agony related to his life not being full of infinite possibilities but rather limited possibilities that were unlike his wishes. He never purchased himself a ticket to internal agony, often finding himself arriving there regardless.

Some days after this Tommy contacted Roscoe but didn't hear back, and Tommy didn't try again. He wasn't visiting Victor in the sitting room either. He didn't hear from anybody or reach out to anybody while his interior self was an uninhabitable desert. So he didn't develop any new work friendships either. He didn't come closer to winning employee of the month. His managers didn't begin to consider promoting him. His managers did remind him to smile.

Most surprising of all, Tommy didn't walk around Woodland Cemetery. But what he did continue doing was walking around his neighborhood, reading, and writing, since they were his life hobbies. One night out alone on the sidewalks in early spring it started raining and he ran back home, feeling inspired by his life and weather enough to write grim poetry he later discarded. When falling inside himself he wrote the words that fell with him. He was reading "In the Heart of the Heart of the Country" by William H. Gass, who was born in North Dakota, bred in Ohio, and died in Missouri; lives in literature forever.

Gass's writing inspired Tommy to expand his emotional perception of his logical self, as all his favorite writing did.

Feeling himself unable to reach what his emotions wanted in life, Tommy couldn't control himself these days.

He and his mother sent each other I Love You texts; she had contracted shingles.

Lucinella texted that she felt bottomed out, wanting to accept reality again; Tommy said he empathized. Lucinella's book about to be published, *Existential Variables*, received a subpar review from *Publishers Weekly*, which fact initially devastated her, but later what calmed her was the *Publishers Weekly* review trashing Dennis Johnson's now-classic *Jesus' Son*. She texted:

    The world is a vampire

And Tommy sure felt her on that.

He was headed toward rock bottom himself, his interior self malfunctioning these days, dark emotions obstructing his vision of reason, feeling like he just can't *life*.

Though everything is up from rock bottom.

Tommy consumed by darkness at his job one day, a manager asked him to step away from the cash register during a slow period, to mop an aisle mess.

Tommy's face expressed dissatisfaction about being asked to do this, but he was at work and it was a manager, so his dissatisfaction further developed while he got the mop bucket.

Tommy did not clean the excessively messy mop bucket, pushing it onto the floor in the same condition as when he found it. The emotional resources from his surroundings did not inspire positive feelings about how things were going, and one of his most destructive accidental tendencies was committing social atrocities while feeling discontent: he mopped with irritation and did a substandard job, looking and behaving like an idiot while feeling pissed; doing a detestable job to manifest his dumb frustration.

Everyone who saw Tommy thought he was overreacting and being melodramatic, they'd seen this before.

Frankly, he looked frightening. A scared customer approached him from having to know, "Where are the green beans?"

Tommy had to swallow his frustrations and fight against his nature in order to respond like a decent person, and point in the general direction.

Spilt ice cream was the mess being mopped, and Tommy missed a big spot by the freezer corner, not dumping out and cleaning the mop bucket after he returned it neither.

So Tommy performed his work tasks while experiencing an internal calamity relating to his perceived life difficulties, but his internal calamity produced further life difficulties, and he further demonstrated himself as problematic. He was asked to mop and felt pissed that it was him who was asked (this was outside his station!), so he responded with absurdity through a faulty perception that kept him on the life path he remained wanting to escape.

The mopping situation spotlighted his professional problem of never motivating anyone to believe him capable of offering anything but frustration, and he returned to the register with a frustrated face, everything feeling frustrating to him: he was being a frustrating person.

Here was how Tommy damaged other people's perception of him: by acting damaged.

This was how interior parts of Tommy made his life more difficult than it needed to be: it wasn't often that people would look at Tommy and see beyond his problems, especially the ones he extensively demonstrated. He could find himself stuck inside himself, which never helped nobody, although this bears repeating: Tommy had more than problems inside himself.

Life is not easy for anyone, and how true it is that life is difficult for difficult people.

There was a moment when Tommy was due for a break, and Monica was supposed to cover him.

Monica was seven years younger than Tommy, and already stronger than he would ever be.

But Monica didn't arrive until after Tommy had begun feeling severely irritated about her tardiness.

She arrived twenty minutes after she was supposed to, without seeming the least bit frustrated about anything. She smiled at Tommy. He couldn't believe she did that; he was mad at her smile. He told the customer at the end of his line, "You're the end of the line." That customer would let in another customer though: how disappointing people were. The new customer had a cart full of cans. Tommy looked up at Monica and her face was a smile with big white teeth. What nerve. Then the customer with the cart full of cans wasn't unloading the cart, wanting until it was their turn to hand each can to Tommy. Tommy didn't have a bagger (the bagger was on a break) so Tommy was bagging the cans he was being handed one-by-one—there were eighty-seven cans, sixteen bags. Tommy's face was passive-aggressive while he attempted to summon witches inside the customer's head like *Exit 666,* but it didn't work because the customer seemed fine. And Monica was still rudely smiling.

Then finally, Tommy in the break room, a manager came up to him and told him to smile.

It was obvious: Tommy should have spent his break outside walking around alone—he'd come to the break room for the community cheesecake. He thought Damn You to his plate with cheesecake crumbs.

Tommy closed his eyes.

The manager said, "Tommy," and Tommy opened his eyes.

Tommy said, "I'm not into smiles today."

The manager sat down across from him, asking what was going on.

Tommy found it difficult to explain his expansive anxieties regarding everything. "It's existential boss, that's all," he couldn't say that.

The manager said Tommy could go home if he needed to.

Tommy felt embarrassed.

Not feeling as if needing to go home.

He apologized, feeling himself the type of person who could work when he had to—wanting his manager to know he would work.

Then, and Tommy had both not expected this and considered it inevitable, the manager said, "Tommy there was a time, about three months ago, when some of your coworkers didn't look forward to seeing you." They had chatted about this during Tommy's yearly review. "You don't like that Tommy either, so let's not see him around."

This deep cut murdered Tommy who wondered again if he could ever become who the world wanted him to be.

His manager's statement was of the variety that initiated Tommy's fight against himself and the world: it had been a long time since one of Tommy's managers believed in him despite his fuck ups—not since his youth had anyone seen him for more than what was wrong with him; so Tommy never believed himself bound for life treasures that weren't promised to him and didn't seem likely in an adult world that called him an obvious problem amid everything else they said about him—being a sane man who believed in himself, he could not accept that rational adult world perspective about him.

Tommy said, "Okay" and nodded.

The manager patted him on the back.

Then the manager said, "And you might want to thank Monica for cleaning the mop bucket." Tommy, wondering what in the hell, locked eyes with his manager. But the manager's face appeared oblivious to the drama involved in the statement. The manager had not meant to sound savage, but reasonable—which felt awful.

Tommy inspected where he'd mopped while returning to the register, feeling glad he at least left behind a tidy spot, not knowing that Monica, the most recent employee of the month, had also mopped the mess he had left behind; and she hadn't even mentioned it to the manager.

Back at this register, Tommy decided not to thank Monica for emptying the mop bucket, which anyone could have done, and she could do it just as easily as he could—he had not been specifically asked to do that, and the mop bucket was dirty before he used it —he hadn't known Monica would be the one who cleaned it up, not having left it behind just for her. Had she volunteered to clean it, or was she asked to? Tommy didn't know why the manager had mentioned this situation to him. He looked over at Monica and she was leaving from her register without looking at him or providing an explanation. He thought Monica was being lame but he knew there were other parts of her too, and he smiled because he knew he couldn't let out a scream; to be fully honest, that means he stayed quiet and smiled while screaming inside himself. And then he understood smiles a different way, feeling reminded that he couldn't understand the full context of everything he experienced each moment.

His fight with life not a riot, he never sought these atrocious situations he often created.

He felt so full of frustration and disappointment he wanted to burst, which he recognized as so outrageous he laughed, which released some pressure.

Maybe his life wasn't as repetitive as him, definitely he couldn't let himself act shocked when his poor decisions led to negative outcomes.

Emotionally speaking Tommy hit rock bottom.

In his dream world literally everything was okay, including when you're not doing things right, but the human world never vibed his dream world from that perspective.

He began thinking about his feelings to make them less confusing, since some things can become less confusing if you really think about it.

In reality it is not accurate to call Tommy a "nobody," the appropriate word is "absurd." He often chose bad decisions before resignation, going the wrong way in order to head somewhere—his reactions to the world his human condition, he realized his mistakes in hindsight and knew if you're better for this world the world is better to you, with certain aspects of a better life based upon contingents; one ritual he had was crossing his fingers to make wishes, not wanting to believe himself truly fucked like his mistakes, resume, and certain outsiders implied.

He and Roscoe had talked about this topic at length in several ways a number of times: "This world says it doesn't need me—I hear there's no good reason for me. So I am a waste of energy but calm down because there's plenty of energy, and my existence need not a reason."

Tommy remembered he only had two hours and thirty more years until he was done with work.

Later he parked his car and walked around his neighborhood, deliberately avoiding feeling worried or thinking too much, only thinking a little about things that didn't worry him too much, such as how the neighborhood was looking that night: the neighborhood looked fine.

There were garbage piles at the end of a Plocher alley, but he figured somebody would eventually clean them up maybe, and they didn't bother him anyway, so if no one picked them up that would be fine too.

It was a Sunday afternoon and Tommy was thinking Not This Again.

This, how many times—too many times, and always the damn same, because of his damn self.

While experiencing a familiar emotional hangover, feeling over feeling worried about himself, Tommy became aware of the fact that to be honest his life was much less worrisome when he stopped worrying about his life so much.

This afternoon he agreed with himself about there being too much awful in the world to fix it all at once, which ignited within him a minor revelation, regarding life requiring slow steps on occasion; and during ensuing days Tommy took slow steps toward restoring secure feelings within the uncertainty of literally everything in life, not denying but preparing to surmount the life hardships he could identify: a normal and healthy life perspective.

He was reading Marcel Proust's *Swann's Way*:

> [...]he told himself that you don't know it when you're unhappy, that you are never as happy as you think.

This line had endnote one-hundred and eight, from translator Lydia Davis, who mentioned the line being adapted from *Maximes,* published anonymously by François, Duc de La Rochefoucauld in 1665, his forty-ninth maxim:

> One is never either as happy or as unhappy as one imagines.

And like usual Tommy experienced strong spiritual magnetism between himself and resonating descriptions of the human condition.

During days of regaining composure amid reality's enormity he began reflecting upon the intricacies of imaginative emotions, rediscovering himself the same as he ever was and would be.

Other people scattered about—playing baseball, playing soccer, just hanging out—Tommy took it easy on a red-and-black checkered flannel blanket, on a grassy hill facing Bomber Park, spectacular afternoon sunlight prompting sunscreen and a green safari hat.

He was reading Grace Paley who, when her eyes became his, instigated metropolitan ideas about expansive perspectives: Tommy further realized that subjectivity can beautify the trivial, and shatter misconceptions about life being dull—no writer worth a penny describes a dull life a dull way.

The abundant park people appeared to be experiencing a swell time while Tommy took breaks from reading Grace Paley to further ponder his common problem with fucking life; he did not feel bitter about lost hopes, no, since he lived off dreams not hopes, and neither did he believe himself to be a prisoner in life which he sometimes acted like.

Investigating his personal problem of acting like a prisoner in life on occasion, over the afternoon he experienced a growing revelation dealing with more than frustrations existing in life; right then Tommy felt far away from frustrations regarding anything—which perspective sounded impossible to him during his frustrated times, but right then felt ethereal, refreshing, and reflective of reality.

After remembering himself incapable of being anybody but himself, during a clean moment of feeling alive and appreciating himself, Tommy was in the mood for his mood to be his reality, even while still not appearing noticeably happy. He wanted the park visitors to be noticeably happy without wanting to be them, and no one wanted to be him either—Tommy felt happy by his own method; everything felt fine.

He returned the blanket and book to his bedroom before strolling his neighborhood sidewalks and thoughts, concocting a plan to reject misery and embrace passion. A couple of times in the past he had investigated embracing passion over misery, chatted about it in full detail with Roscoe, and written mental Post-it notes regarding, so this late-afternoon his experienced self began devising a long-term plan to carry this idea through inevitable future rough life patches—not truly able to picture smoother days ahead of him, for a little while Tommy imagined his future becoming what he couldn't imagine.

That night alone in his room he listened to soothing music that pleased him; life hardships not sounding so bad depending on how you make them sound. He experienced significant emotional bonding with Fats Waller singing Andy Razaf lyrics for "Ain't Misbehavin." The song is about feeling content while being alone, and waiting for someone you haven't met yet. Fats Waller and Andy Razaf reminded Tommy that he wasn't alone being alone, so he didn't feel alone while being alone and listening to their song about the topic.

Much fuss is often made regarding people feeling alone around others, such fuss was made in this book for example, but being mentioned right now is feeling together with others while being alone, like what happened between Tommy and Fats Waller and Andy Razaf for example.

Next Tommy listened to Billie Eilish, whom he could appreciate without relating to. She was seventeen then, listened to by millions, toured the globe, began on SoundCloud, and wrote songs with her brother, who was a solo musician too: raw young people making fascinating contemporary music that Tommy found compelling.

The next morning Tommy awoke to a brand new history: different from the rest but with strong similarities. It being true that the reality of yesterday no longer existed, today Tommy decided not to feel as if missing out on anything in life, though other people might disagree, including Tommy on another day, still no one including himself wanted to hear his complaints today: another day when he felt himself able to see his life another way.

He allowed himself to believe that everything was going well even though it didn't seem like it. If it was all going horribly wrong still it was going okay, and please understand that he did not desire to scream throughout his entire life; maybe-doomed Tommy desired to invent marvelous personal illusions in a world already filled with an abundance of the reasonable that always displeased him.

After a work shift he returned to his room without leaving it for the remainder of the evening because he felt fine being alone doing nothing. On his navy blue futon he absorbed life experience through lonely light memories, entering an inner haven unobstructed by adult world demands; some call this "relaxing."

Momentarily to Tommy his life felt like nothing more than time, and he aspired for nothing more than life—feeling fine headed nowhere, not feeling the need to head somewhere, no sense of urgency right then, his worries didn't matter while he didn't have them for a short while, blissing out on nothingness and floating across the ocean of time.

His following days were as alike as one drop of water to another, which Devashish related to after hearing about. It became another new day in another new month with similar new things and, open to his life's not-much-of-anything, Tommy searched for meaning within books, daydreams, and his thoughts along his neighborhood streets: McClain to Keowee, a right on Bacon, a right on Dutoit, left on 5th, right on McClure, all the way down to Webbland, which changes into Allen—spring rain ending, thankfully, since there had been too many rainstorms at the end of spring, summer now beginning and the sun setting later, calmer and warmer weather arriving, Tommy multi-tasked his life hobbies by off-and-on reading Emmanuel Bove's *My Friends* while walking—a left on Xenia, he walked until dinnertime and then he walked again, past sunset, waving to his grandmother on an waning gibbous moon—a long walk headed nowhere, bringing him back to a burgundy velvet chaise longue, and Victor on a grey elegantly upholstered wing chair by an open window, with Bea Lillie singing "There Are Times."

They were listening to Broadway show tunes in the sitting room one late-spring early-evening when Tommy asked Victor, "What do you think when I say that life is hard?"

And for a short while Victor didn't reply, then asking Tommy the reason for asking the question, prompting Tommy to mention some emotional tribulations he was struggling overcoming and not in the mood to talk about actually.

Victor soaked this in before replying, "Life is good, it's the work that's hard."

Nice.

Though to Tommy, much of his life felt not hard but unnecessary, with every little thing seeming to get in the way of the big thing he wanted and could never find—this was why he evaded the low-hanging fruits on the tree of life known as small talk.

During a lonely late-evening sidewalk stroll, Tommy looked up at the dots of light in the sky and contemplated not being a fan of small talk seriously. And life provides the natural resources for immense small talk—a quality of life that bothered Tommy.

Another day, unrelated, Tommy experienced an unfortunate episode of strep throat, followed by severely outlandish hemorrhoids.

Next his ears became clogged by cerumen and with a bulb syringe he blew out an eardrum by accident: undesirable. Then he realized that with regularity he was grinding his teeth while sleeping, based on his jaw and teeth feeling sore in his mornings, and four or five years prior he wore a fitted dental guard, but he could not find again what he must have lost, and he couldn't afford a dentist now, so he ended up store buying an adjustable mouthguard that swivels to fit your bite.

None of this was entertaining, none of it was meaningful, and all of it was only some of all that happened. His car started breaking down, causing him to panic about the future of his car and finances (Omar related). He ended up selling his busted-up old car for one-thousand dollars, and buying a new used car for four thousand. Its purchase drained his savings account, but this was why he had the savings account in the first place. Except: now he didn't have a savings account. Then his cell phone *and* laptop broke, and he had to replace these expensive necessities by opening a second credit card. A new monthly premium.

Why did things like this happen?

Because life kept happening, and he would not ask: why did life keep happening? Although now and then he did ask that. He lived check to check, every purchase feeling like an emergency, making life choice readjustments while considering book or movie ticket purchases, he was familiar with burdensome circumstances of his fiscal reality. At this point in time he had quit buying cigarettes because he couldn't afford the addiction. He quit drinking caffeine after concluding it nonessential and overrated. His rent payment system: Tommy paid his rent to the housekeeper Tabitha. Tommy's rent became Tabitha's salary, allowing Victor both to avoid the money issue and make it urgent, which adult world strategy Tommy recognized. This crafty system worked since Tabitha needed the money Victor didn't. Victor hadn't figured out the whole wide world but he'd figured out how to be a boss.

Tommy didn't have money for buying a bed, he slept on a navy blue futon that's been mentioned. He wished for vacations but where would he go, and with whom, and plus how much would it cost—he seldom traveled, never traveled far (he'd never traveled over an ocean), only taking brief trips down to Cincinnati or visiting his cousins in the country on occasion, his landscapes mostly limited to Dayton; yet he desired to see the world in all the ways it could be seen— everything was fine—what he did was explore the landscapes offered by books, encountering other life perspectives by reading, experiencing the world outside his own through writers with gorgeous perspectives spanning time and culture.

His remedy to the adult world was art culture, and all this was all true while it all happened as time kept going, with Tommy going along with time as well as he could. As a child he learned that one keeps going through whatever, but over his time alive he became aware of all the whatever that one keeps going through. The writer is confessing that certain information is being given less preference to this book compared to the emotional dimensions of Tommy's existence. Certain many other details of Tommy's life are being omitted since many life details felt to him like white noise over the songs of his dreams, and this book wants to feel like Tommy.

Tommy's daily calibrations about his endless anxieties regarding every aspect of reality, in addition to his overall lack of any type of certainty: what the fuck did this mean in relation to the person he was—solid question, healthy curiosity; desiring to feel content while stuck being himself, Tommy discovered who he was by writing, becoming who he was meant to be.

One Tommy quality was he didn't just like books, he felt they mattered—they mattered to him—writers were his overall-dearest long distance friends—and he learned what literature could do in order to do it himself. He was on a path toward almost-beginning to write his next book, still conceptualizing, still turning his ideas in his cognitive wheelhouse, knowing for certain that his book would be titled *City of Flowers and Sunshine*, and about him as his same self but living in Los Angeles. He would be the same person someplace else, comfortably alive in the free and easy skies of the goddamn make believe. He familiarized himself with Los Angeles street names using Google Maps, preparing himself to behave exactly as if in Dayton. And with his intended narrative plan he knew that some readers might think 'the protagonist often walks alone—gross,' but Tommy intended to implement an emotional procedure that would maybe inspire people to think 'I've never adored anything as much as this fucking guy adores lonely strolls and reading.'

Always wanting to write a book he would want to read, also Tommy was intending to write a book that somebody needed to write. He felt amped about writing his book that nobody was waiting to read, and while thinking about who he was he began wondering if he didn't try to become himself so much as all he could ever tolerate was being himself, despite how not helpful that often was.

During the important part of beginning to write *City of Flowers and Sunshine*, thinking about it, his ideas coalescing, he was listening to Helado Negro's "Seen My Aura" when Alexander texted him a photo of a dog sitting in a car.

Tommy texted back the revolving hearts emoji.

And then while feeling emotionally centered on a Wednesday afternoon for a variety of reasons, Tommy crossed paths with Omar leaving from work.

Tommy the one who wanted to talk today, Omar stopped and made eye contact, ready to listen.

And after hearing Tommy speak about further noticing his personal flaws that manifested in his adult reality, Omar said, "Hey."

Tommy said, "Yeah what?"

Omar said, "You should text Maha."

Omar smiled when Tommy looked at him.

Tommy said, "Text her what?"

Omar shuffled his feet while glancing at the sky, looking back at Tommy and saying, "Tell her I'm asking you to text her."

So Tommy texted this to Maha before driving home.

And back in his room, on his navy blue futon, for spiritual healing purposes he was reading poems in Gregory Kan's *Under Glass*:

> Stay with me
> because I am just about ready to exist.

He had forgotten about the text he sent Maha, but then he remembered. His phone was on silent. He picked it up and the screen lit up, there were notifications, he read the notifications about the texts from Maha:

    publishing guy, friend of a friend

    a nice guy who's visiting

    upcoming event for a local artist everyone knows

    you're invited xx

A starry moonless sky above the blacktop parking lot of a suburban strip mall, mild streetlamp light pollution.

Across the street: Centerville's number one laser tag facility, and an admirable mini-golf course.

A franchise furniture store behind him, Tommy walked toward a franchise seafood restaurant, cater-cornered to a local pizza parlor and jewelry store.

Everything vacant of the unusual, this suburban environment did not bother Tommy, who believed reality to be so enormous that no matter where or who you are you're tiny—he spent the vast majority of his time and effort ruminating upon aspects of life regarding the human condition, not this shit.

This environment that might have lacked a certain spark, it did possess a certain spirit, and a spark vanishes while a spirit persists—Tommy figured that out following [the fire going out on all his relationships that began with a spark] figuring out that anybody can figure out a way to love what they want to love. This environment's spirit came not from places but people—it was a whole lot of nothing special that everybody here considered more than enough.

On this late-summer Friday evening Tommy entered a restaurant he never visited except that was a lie since there he was and, instantaneously, for a damn good reason, he appreciated his immersion within the atmosphere of casual seafood dining.

The special occasion: his father's sixty-seventh birthday.

On special occasions Tommy crossed paths with his father's side of the family, though he was further acquainted with his mother's side, since she raised him. But Tommy was Midwestern enough to appreciate both sides, and fortunate enough that no one in his whole family was a fundamentally terrible person.

The restaurant crowded, cacophonous, reservations not made, big tables occupied, Tommy sat at the open end of a two-person table pushed against a four-person table beside a wall at the dining room's middle: his aunt Abigail, uncle Gerald, and their son cousin Alan sat to his right nearest to furthest, his father, mamaw, and cousin-in-law Patty sat to his left.

Mamaw: Appalachian idiomatic, means grandmother, connected to Tommy's cultural identity his family told him.

And the roots of both sides of his family tree did indeed disappear inside multi-cultural Appalachian soil: he was Thomas Gavin Campbell and his surname was Scottish, his mother's maiden name was

Polish, although neither side was pure Scottish or Polish. Some English and German and whatnot too. Once a DNA fact check revealed his mother's side was not partially Native American like Tommy had been informed they were. They were not quite sure about their deepest roots, neither side of his family able to fully describe their cultural selves, anyway Tommy certainly did not and could not be bothered by who he already was, however sordid he seemed— multiple-times he referred to himself as an 'American mongrel' but that had not become popular among anybody, he was thinking about auditioning 'human cocktail' instead—longing for the title of a memorable sideshow performer, all Tommy knew was his self-complexity operated under multitudinous conditions to his utter torment and delight.

Anyway when Tommy looked at his family he observed bright hot spots within a cold dark reality, since no one and nothing looks better than when they or it look like love to you, and that's the only kind of bias that's worth a damn. There at the casual seafood restaurant for a family affair, following a standard conversational routine regarding changing years and weather, shifting sunset timeslots, menu possibilities, observations about special menu items, and ordering their food, settling comfortably, then, for probably the same simple reason as always ('polite' curiosity), aunt Teresa brought up a topic that Tommy wasn't in the mood to dwell upon, even under these circumstances, asking him, "Darling, how are you?"

Apparently shit out of luck; her dreaded conversational opener desires not veracity but positivity—Tommy was thirty-five years old and still disinterested in giving reasonable social responses to the standard question of how he was doing. Within his nonstandard feelings he felt fine enough to not feel the need to talk about how he felt, exiting Teresa's question by replying, "Everything's fine, thanks," and nodding with a smile that meant Maybe Don't Push Me.

But Teresa didn't register his smile's intention and pushed him, asking, "Oh, what's going on?"

Oof-uck; Tommy longed for this conversation to arrive at any topic not related to him, but he did not explode, no instead he jumped straight into a summary by saying, "I'm a part-time cashier who won't be promoted. I'm writing books no one reads. That's how I am."

He had not really wanted his family to hear that.

Tommy thought his life only sounded bad; he hoped his nonexistent romantic life wouldn't be called into question. A person on the other side of the restaurant erupted into a coughing fit for unrelated reasons before Teresa said, "Okay well, thanks for mentioning, because how would I know unless you tell me?"

Tommy in fact learned from his father how to respond to basic personal questions (make it apparent that you don't know how to begin), but wishing to retreat from his situation he employed a cheery tone while asking his father, "What's new with you?"

And first his father laughed as if having heard a profoundly good joke before saying all he said, which was, "Nothing new going on here." Totally: still a retired truck driver who had worked four jobs since then, graveyard shifts at drug stores and Walmart, without a current job.

Respecting his father's succinct reply about nothing new going on with him, but again avoiding being asked another basic question himself, Tommy asked his father, "Do you want another job?"

His father said, "Well, yeah," before small laughter suggested a personal belief in that question being the definition of hilarious.

"A job gives you something to do in the day," Tommy noted.

"Gives my day a reason," his father agreed.

"What kind of job you thinking about?"

"A driving job. I miss driving."

Motion. Tommy craved the motion of emotion and, having become the conversation leader through sheer misfortune, just for kicks he asked, "How are you, mamaw?"

Husky bird-like laughter fluttered from her mouth before she said all she said, "Feeling fine today."

Tommy truly was not bothered by dead-end conversations, both understanding and relating to this social dynamic, but tables tend to feel the need for conversation, for reasons with which Tommy did not agree: people needing to be somebody, rather than enter pure states of being. Okay so Tommy just sat there and thankfully, what a relief, on her own Patty began talking about how she and Alan were doing.

They were doing about the same as always, life plain being what they experienced while making their own way and feeling fine; a longer explanation of the shorter replies. But then Alan broadened the conversation by cracking open specifics, mentioning certain personal experiences obtained through his parks and recreation job. Followed by Teresa saying she was proud of Alan for being a fantastic worker. After which Patty agreed plus added he was a fabulous father too (their son Adam at his first slumber party).

Even with his family Tommy could often feel as if living on another planet than most people. Only two years older than Tommy, the lives and perspectives of Patty and Alan were far different than his; a blood relative, Alan would not have described a shared planet from anywhere near the same perspective as Tommy.

Patty was discussing Adam's recent baseball accomplishments when the food arrived, and regular conversations continued over casual dining; Tommy listened while eating maple-glazed chicken. Thinking outside the box for no good reason, he had wanted to see how the chicken tasted at this seafood restaurant —and it tasted maple-glazed; he had zero complaints.

There was lobster on everybody elsc's plates.

A lengthy sports discussion was followed by a heavenly pocket of conversational silence, inside of which Tommy felt his calmest. Until the quietness he treasured began worrying him—someone might confuse his calmness with being open to questions. Others feared the silence and he feared the questions. Except Teresa, thank God, began sharing stories from a recent family vacation.

"During a medieval duel we drank from goblets."

They had been to Florida and Patty mentioned, "Manatees became my fourth favorite living creatures."

Alan described air boating across the everglades, and shared a handful of interesting alligator facts. Tommy felt relieved they were talking amongst themselves, if they felt the need to talk. Without a job story he wanted to share, and only knowing a handful of greatest accomplishments that everyone knew regarding sports, plus not having been on a recent vacation, Tommy felt more than happy continuing to listen.

And the evening strolled along at a leisurely pace when this fantastic surprise occurred: after the meal but before the check, without clowning around Tommy's father asked anybody, "Why are we here?"

"Why not?" Teresa asked, having organized this.

Ah Teresa, here was a question for you.

"Well, it's not where I would've selected for my birthday!" His father said.

Tommy laughed first, because of the extraordinary circumstances. But Teresa appeared unfazed and said, "We came here for your birthday last year!"

Tommy felt flabbergasted.

His father made a flummoxed face, "Did we?"

Teresa said, "I've got pictures!"

Teresa brought out her phone, found a picture, and handed the phone to her brother.

His father titled back his head to laugh.

The laughter proved contagious as the phone was passed around, everybody laughed, and Tommy had laughed the whole while, but his final laugh was for a different reason than his first. He smiled at Teresa before a surprise occurred to everybody not him: six waiters arrived to sing Tommy's personal request, "For He's a Jolly Good Fellow," which nobody can deny. He had told their waiter, "You know what'll be cool?" But while it was being sung Tommy wasn't sure if it was cool or awkward; it seemed to lean toward awkward. This was not his first time experiencing this sensation. Everybody sang along, but nobody gave it their all.

"Well huh, how about that," Patty said after the waiters departed.

It seemed as if everybody felt relieved the song was over.

And Mamaw—who saw this coming, maybe nobody, maybe everybody but Tommy—anyway she started singing "Happy Birthday to You."

Patty, Alan, Teresa and Gerald jumped right in.

Then Tommy did too (he played his own game but was not against the games of others).

Secretly Tommy felt positive about being able to soon leave this place.

And next he felt relaxed on a flowered yellow polyester couch in his mamaw's tv room, with his mamaw and father on midnight blue plush recliners facing a cathode ray tube tv. On the tv was a simple crime show unrelated to the type of shows that people were serious about in critical and award show context those days. His mamaw and father followed along because why not it's fun okay. Tommy didn't listen or pay attention except to scare himself now and then, feeling as if paying attention to tv inspired garbage dreams. What tv shows seemed to manifest was wasted time he felt, though escapism comes to different people in different forms. Tommy was more into the internet for pop culture, and books for fresh passions; not the quality of the tv show, but the quality of its memes.

So while ignoring the show that felt unrelated to his own sense of being, and holding a glass of strawberry lemonade in one hand, meanwhile Tommy felt himself inside a room that felt inside of him— this tv room felt important to him, like his family and life felt important to him, for various solid reasons difficult to concretely explain. This room had seen Tommy grow as a person, his mamaw having lived in this house his entire life.

Ninety-three year-old mamaw was his oldest-living family member. His mother's mother he called grandmother died of heart failure and moved to the moon; his mother's father died of pancreatic cancer; and lung cancer killed papaw, who had been a smoker and a carpenter. Mamaw quit smoking after her one true love died, but Tommy's father continued smoking, once saying, "You know, some people can smoke and they'll be okay, and I think I've smoked long enough to know I'll be okay," believing that smoking had chosen not to kill him; Tommy shared all of his father's wishes, though they both knew themselves bound to what happens.

Mamaw's life reminded Tommy that life happens and can keep happening; his whole family reminded him that one makes one's way however one does— however your life goes is the way it goes, best not to overthink all the bad stuff that arrives on its own.

Back in his book-and-movie-hoarded bedroom at the end of his day, awake but with his eyes closed, on his navy blue futon Tommy reflected upon the strength of his mamaw and mother having inspired his personal development in pivotal ways. Then he reflected upon the life paths his parents had taken: each of them past the age of retirement then, each with little money, each single—they had never married each other, never been in love with each other, Tommy had never been meant to be—their lives had not been easy, though despite what others might say their lives were always more than worth it to Tommy who loved both his parents, and the world

doesn't work on love alone yet still, love works; this
thought drifted into his sleep that night.

His mother was speaking about the book fair over the phone, "Yeah I figured out that it's a game—it's a game, okay—because I am the person who won the main prize last year, and this year I didn't win anything. But. The person who won the year before me hasn't won since then either. And not the person from the year before that person either. They let the new people win so they will come back to win again —that's their breeding pattern.

"Once you've won you're done, unless you're local.

"The people who live near the book fair are a close-knit group of friends."

Tommy mentioned, "Huh, well—now you can feel motivated to think about your writing existing outside the book fair."

His mother said, "A professional self-help writer encouraged me to unpublish my self-published books, and edit them for submission to a professional publisher. He says that publishing to Amazon doesn't do anything."

It was afternoon and Tommy was out walking around, headed across East Fifth Avenue while listening to his mother. Their conversation concluded, he then read his daily advice from his astrological app:

Document your good ideas.

Oh, wow. This app that didn't know Tommy could speak to him as if it did, and support him in a few critical ways. He read that his day's power was in:

thinking & creativity.

Which felt extraordinarily uplifting of his astrological app to mention.

Next on Instagram, through a random page recommendation, Tommy read a meme with a motivational perspective unattributed to anybody:

To refuse the risk is to refuse the reward.

And hell yes: that night Tommy began rewriting the first paragraph of *City of Flowers and Sunshine*, having rewritten this first paragraph a hundred-thousand times previously, this time he implemented a divine thrust.

Followed by Tommy finishing reading *King Lear* for inspirational writing purposes. After recently rewatching the adaptation of Herman Melville's *Pierre: or, The Ambiguities,* Leos Carax's *Pola X*, then via Wikipedia Tommy read about the multidimensional wordsmith William Shakespeare having inspired the writing in Melville's grandest novel that absolutely everybody had heard about by Tommy's time, *Moby-Dick; or, The Whale*.

In terms of which *King Lear* character Tommy hoped he was, he hoped he was one of the good people, despite his complicated fragility perhaps omitting him from the clarity of vision involved in being a good person. He hoped he was more like Edgar than Edmund; he would feel content being The Fool:

> I had rather be any kind o' thing than a fool:
> and yet I would not be thee, nuncle.

Having never been here before, Tommy still sensed himself on a planet where people lived beneath a dome.

Unafraid of anything right then, only the night and the city existing, Tommy walked through an alley's scattered lamplights, headed toward the glow of a street.

A hand of his was shaped like a fist the size of his heart when Tommy heard the question, "Feeling worthless, hopeless? Does your good life feel impossible?"

Sure he could feel that way but he hadn't been right then, except now he was; he glanced around wondering from where the voice came.

"You can feel another way," the voice said.

Well, he had felt different before being asked those questions, Tommy thought.

He emerged from the alley into vibrant city street lights, and luminous reflections off towering glass skyscrapers. It was late-late and Tommy was alone with his own reflection, the voice now saying, "Your same life with a new feeling, you can do it, think about it," and Tommy looked above and below himself, in a full circle around himself, searching for the source of the voice before realizing he was speaking to himself.

Next a bronze horse bust was in front of his eyes, the burgundy velvet chaise longue beneath him, and while sitting up Tommy's thoughts returned to reality, aspects of himself still beneath the dome.

He compared the dome dream to when he was a blue orb of light, deciding he cherished them equally.

In this scenario Victor had fallen asleep too, on the grey elegantly upholstered wing chair by the open window.

Was Victor dreaming right then?

If he was dreaming, what wasn't he dreaming about—as in, was he dreaming about everything?

After replying to an emoji of a man farmer with an emoji of a badger, then Tommy texted Lucinella regarding being about to cross paths with this publishing person who was apparently an editor.

Lucinella verbalized hope and Tommy stayed cool by texting he would see what might happen; Lucinella related and mentioned her own night plan of sunset motorcycling.

Then the rest of the world seemed frigid compared to hellacious hot Omar and Maha: in a slick black and white suit, shiny black shoes, and a fabulous deep-blue bow tie, dressed-his-best Omar was a stunner; and where had Maha learned to shape her hair like that, from where had she purchased her mad chic dress, plus her phenomenal earrings, genuinely wow —Tommy had never seen his good friends look this fire.

Tommy wore a thrifty top-buttoned indigo collared shirt with floral designs, maroon acid washed jeans and yellow sneakers.

A sudden brief and not too surprising extrapolation on the topic of Tommy's opinion about his physical reality, to further illuminate his interior self, dig this: all the previously-mentioned and overabundant existential worries that exhausted Tommy, well, he possessed identical dimensional worries relating to his corporeality, like how pretty and intelligent he was; in any given normal room there were prettier and more intelligent people than Tommy who was aging, his hair, teeth, mind and everything about his body changing, his style transforming, and who had he been in the first place —which equals a whole bunch of facts that Tommy contemplated so often he could overcontemplate them, sometimes thinking himself to heaven and sometimes thinking himself to hell; he was uniquely human, the same as many others and yet so often feeling alone: human condition.

The party was at a downtown Cincinnati warehouse a short drive away, and Tommy's plan was to absorb the night rather than project interior landscapes of nervous ideation. No fibbing: from the backseat and with the car windows down, the music loud, Tommy experienced a teenage-like buzz of anticipation regarding the night's tremendous possibilities. Was not this party his chance to be among others who consider the feelings that come from art as vital as the feelings that come from life— maybe. Perhaps.

His hand surfed the nighttime wind outside a window, his other hand Shazammed the current song playing, which turned out to be "Black Balloons Reprise" by Flying Lotus featuring Denzel Curry.

Maha placed her hand atop Omar's hand and earlier Tommy had noticed slight tension between them, but her body behavior suggested tensions were being released, which Tommy classified as adorable.

They arrived at an expansive vaulted loft with five spaced out floor lamps—one lamp in each corner, and one in the room's center; dirty concrete floors and windows facing adjacent buildings; poems scrawled across white walls in black paint; and around forty people of various races, sexual orientations, body sizes and gender complexities, three of whom Tommy had learned about over Instagram, at this event for non-conformist and non-binary artist types.

The event's star was a supreme painter able to pay for her life through art: she lived in a Kentucky suburb, was single, and comprehended a painterly technique that many admired, with thousands of Instagram followers. But the attendee whom Tommy most heard talked about among party goers was the most successful: a Scottish investigative journalist shooting a Netflix documentary about feeling thunderstruck by facts.

Tommy most adored an accomplished Salvadoran musician who was in his normal mood of not worrying about anything in his excellent life, his Bahraini transgender mixed media artist girlfriend the sweetest person imaginable. Everybody being themselves, everybody was different from everybody else, the art world overall non-anything except for everything, everybody at this party shared a spiritual vibrancy expressed by fashion that Tommy would have had to Google for a vigorous half hour to describe.

So everybody was awesome, but in truth the event was not easy as always, for the standard reason that people were involved. Nearly being an event related to essential meaning, not all the conversations felt very essential, to be blunt not any—no one speaking about expansive ideas or their true feelings. Truth be told Tommy detected a self-aware party atmosphere that felt dissimilar to typical Midwestern parties. Most everybody was relaxed but therapy related, and still there was a particular kind of unspoken nervous energy in fabulous looking people speaking about where they had traveled in the world, with Tommy longing to hear about the world inside of them.

Everybody can see the same shared reality, but only each person can see what they dream, and Tommy most desired what could only come from each person. Life gets in the way of being able to express life, Fernando Pessoa said, and he was quite right.

Not feeling more comfortable than usual in an art world environment, and believing that dreams were the only way the universe could be remade, Tommy monitored his cognitive biases totally, in particular his bias blind spot, trait ascription bias, extrinsic incentives bias, introspection illusion, and attribution bias. To be honest when he read the tone of the room with a perspective devoid of melodrama, looking at reality as he did following one of his emotional tragedies—not horrible and not great, regular—still he did not see how he could fit in here better than anyplace else.

Not even fun new cool topics like deep ecology or biohacking were being discussed—whatever this place wanted wasn't Tommy, who was standing alone thinking about the snow leopard when Maha grabbed his elbow, leading him across the room.

He knew it must be the editor they were headed toward, and in the corner he saw the person whom that might be: tall, handsome, dependable looking, with a kind hearted face, wearing an ocean blue business shirt and a red tie, red pants and white business shoes.

Tommy began inducing himself with positive remembrances regarding his personal accomplishments: his poetry book of writerly innocence; his underrated singular memoir; and the novel he was beginning.

Different than he expected, Maha and Tommy arrived at the side of the room, among a group of three people standing between lamps, half in the light and half in the dark. Maha gestured toward a short bald man with a black mustache, wearing a torn black t-shirt, blue denim jeans and black sneakers. She said, "Fernando, Tommy. Tommy, Fernando."

Fernando said, "Hi Tommy."

"Hi."

Tommy smiled after Fernando did.

Maha stepped between the two other people and Fernando, saying, "Hi, I'm Maha," and holding out her hand to one of them, smiling at the other who would be next, providing Tommy with an opportunity.

Unsure about what might happen, Tommy was certain *something* would happen; he felt *nervous*.

"Tell me about yourself," Fernando said with a smile.

It was a basic prompt that shook Tommy who said, "Huh? Oh. Great to meet you. I walk around alone at night, haha, and I write."

Still-smiling Fernando said, "What do you write?"

"I'm writing a book about myself if I lived in Los Angeles, *City of Flowers and Sunshines.*"

Continuing to smile, Fernando said, "What will you do in Los Angeles?"

Tommy said, "Live," and that was all. He waited to see if Fernando thought that was a good one or not.

Fernando nodded.

Fernando hadn't mentioned his job. He hadn't done anything but ask questions that steered to this moment when Tommy wondered what Fernando knew and thought about him.

Tommy added, "I'll walk around, read and write like I do in real life, but I'll live in Los Angeles. Um. Anyway it's a mental landscape of a book, with transcendental riddles."

Fernando had entered nodding territory. His diverted eyes scanned the back of the room. Tommy wondered if Fernando could see inside of Tommy who wasn't much of a conversationalist in terms of being able to explain himself, hoping Fernando realized and forgave him, which would be easier if Fernando agreed with Tommy that deeper truths lie beneath what a person can even think to say. Was Tommy's spirit glowing or what? Would being only himself be enough for right then? Would it help if he began describing his emotions?

Fernando put his hand on Maha's back, who turned around, and he kissed her on the cheek. "I've been waved to, " he said, turning to Cheshire grin at Tommy and saying, "You understand," before heading to the room's far side.

Bewildered Tommy watched it all happen.

Maha stepped toward Tommy and shrugged, placing her hand on his.

Moments later she said, "Oh…no."

Almost viciously obviously, in a tragically short amount of time Fernando was out the front door with another person.

Maha squeezed Tommy's hand. She said, "Not on my watch," and headed to the shut door she opened and stepped outside, leaving the door open behind her.

If nightmare realities didn't want to exhaust Tommy they should pace themselves! It would be unfair to say that he was the one being melodramatic here. None of his epiphanies about feeling positive cured his current apprehension. All he knew for sure was he would include a story about this in *City of Flowers and Sunshine.*

Though none of his writing ideas, nor his life related beliefs and worries, could change what would happen while he waited alone in a dark spot between floor lamps.

www.ingramcontent.com/pod-product-compliance
Lightning Source LLC
Chambersburg PA
CBHW020751250626
47155CB00003B/1029